BROKEN
KING

Like Alan Garner, P   fairy-
tales out searching for   magic,
and turns it into a haunting adventure exploring love,
cour e, fear and friendship. Written with sensitivity,
intelligence and conviction, it's the kind of classic story
readers can't get enough of.

– Amanda Craig

Ech   with references to all kinds of mythologies,
jumping effortlessly between Greek gods and the
Brothers Grimm, with a classy dash of Victorian gothic.
The roken King is superbly written and totally gripping,
and I want the next bit now.

– Kate Saunders, Literary Review

A cracking pace, enigmatic characters and terrifying
adve aries will have you clamouring for the next in the series.

– Sarah Naughton

Con e[s] an eerie poetry of the subconscious, a kind of
Alice in Terrorland.

– SF, Financial Times

Philip Womack's new, uncompromising fantasy adventure *The Broken King* flies intoxicatingly through a vividly imagined, treacherous and magical world. It's been loved by our Kids Reader Reviewers and our own Julia Eccleshare. It's perfect family reading and, what's more, it's the first in a planned series. Happy days!

— Love Reading 4 Kids

Mesmorising fantasy . . . this page-turner of a novel grips throughout and will have the reader keen to read the rest of the trilogy.

— Parents in Touch

Simon sets off on a mission to rescue [his sister] and finds himself caught up in an extraordinary and fantastical world in which it is impossible for him to predict what will happen next . . . A magical story full of powerful images and unexpected consequences.

— Julia Eccleshare

[Womack] leads his characters through situations and worlds, both familiar and fantastical, in weird and wonderful ways. There's a definite sense of Arthurian legends and fantasy writing which is no surprise as Womack is a big fan of the works of TH White and Ursula Le Guin.

— We Love This Book

The Broken King [is] the first in *The Darkening Path* series – a set of books steeped in magic, where people transform into swans, doorways to other worlds open up beneath supermarkets and artefacts in the British Museum hold very special powers . . . Womack even managed to make drinking a cappuccino creepy!

– Abi Elphinstone (moontrug)

This was an exhilarating, dark adventure which kept me hooked from the first page to the last word. The creatures were terrifying and amazing. Fantastic!

– Sam Harper, age 10, Love Reading 4 Kids

FANTASTICALLY written fantasy adventure, from the day it arrived it didn't leave my hands. It will capture your imagination from the very first page. I can't wait for book two to be published.

– Rose Heathcote, age 15, Love Reading 4 Kids

Plenty of horror, plenty of monsters, lots of action – everything the young fantasy reader will love. Described as for the 11+ reader, it will be enjoyed by any competent reader as our two young protagonists set out on a quest of atonement to try to retrieve their siblings.

– The Mole, ourbookreviewsonline

For
For Olivia Breese & Julia Finch

Also available in
The Darkening Path trilogy:

The Broken King

Also by Philip Womack

The Other Book
The Liberators

THE DARKENING PATH
BOOK TWO

THE
KING'S
SHADOW

Philip Womack

troika books

Published by TROIKA BOOKS

First published 2015

Troika Books

Well House, Green Lane, Ardleigh CO7 7PD, UK

www.troikabooks.com

A CIP catalogue record for this book is available

from the British Library

ISBN 978-1-909991-12-5

1 2 3 4 5 6 7 8 9 10

Printed in Poland

CONTENTS

꧁ ꧂

Chapter One

IN THE LAND OF
THE BROKEN KING

'QUICK!' SIMON GASPED, and pulled Flora down behind an outcrop of dark rocks that rose along the side of the road they'd tumbled on to. 'Get down! Soldiers are coming!'

They'd only gone a few paces from where they'd fallen through the hole in the fabric of the universe into the land of the Broken King. Simon turned to check if the gap was still there. It was, and for a brief moment he saw through it into the forest clearing in Sussex. There, lit by the moon of a different world, was their friend Giles Cuthbertson, collapsed on his knees.

Giles stirred, noticed them, and began to scramble

forwards. Just as he reached the gap, it closed.

There was no sign it had ever been there.

The portal home had slammed shut; how they would open it again, they had no idea.

'Well, that's that, then . . .' said Flora.

Simon suddenly realised he could see Flora. 'We're not invisible any more. The shadow's gone!'

'I bet it doesn't last between worlds,' said Flora. 'More importantly, how are we going to get back?'

Simon thought quickly. 'The shadow-spheres – we've each got two left. And we've still got the hunting horn and the sunsword. They got us here, and they might get us back. But let's not think about that now. Look!' It was getting lighter as a silver sun rose above them, casting an eerie light and bringing some small warmth with it.

It must be a star, thought Simon. *We must be on a different planet. A different world , or galaxy, maybe, or even dimension . . .*

They were in a small, stony depression by a shining black road; jagged rocks were strewn all around them. In the distance, to the north-west there rose the black glass towers of a walled city, banners and pennants fluttering from the crenellations.

To their left, pouring across the barren, dark

plain that stretched towards the city, was a company of about a hundred soldiers led by a mounted, armed knight with metal wings on either side of his helmet. On their right, a cart drawn by what seemed to be a horse was moving slowly along the road towards the city.

'Where's Pike?' whispered Simon, a little cowed by the sight of the armed men. 'Did he follow us here? *Could* he follow us?'

A splutter made them turn, and there, partly concealed by a jutting stone shard, and lying on his back, was the pale, black-haired boy who'd rescued them from danger so many times.

Flora pulled nervously at Simon's sleeve and they ran to him. Pike's eyes were closed and he wasn't moving. Flora pinched his cheek, but he made no sign of feeling it, although he was breathing shallowly. Simon remembered the bottle of water in his rucksack, found it and splashed him, but Pike did not stir.

They made him as comfortable as they could, resting his head against a smooth rock behind a small ridge where he was shielded from the wind and anyone who might pass on the road, and went back to their post. Here they could see over the plain. A little distance away from where they crouched was a standing stone, the twin of the one they'd come from in their own world. Beyond that was a small stream, which wound its way past them, rushing to join a larger river that flowed towards the south. Hills surrounded the whole area, rising towards mountains whose white peaks seemed to merge into the sky. Strange birds with white rings around their eyes and red beaks boomed and called overhead. Their edges were blurry and shadowy, like the shadow-snake Simon and Flora had fought a few days before.

Dominating everything was the city. A turreted wall ran round the whole thing, with its black towers soaring upwards, light glinting off their glass sides. Two larger towers rose from the centre of the city, marking a starkly outlined fortified citadel on top of a low hill.

'So this is it,' said Flora. 'We're in the land of the Broken King. And I thought it only existed in a book for children . . . But it's real, all of it. And the Broken King's got Johnny.' She rubbed her nose with the sleeve of her brother's leather jacket. 'And Anna.'

Simon assessed the situation quickly. The soldiers were now formed in a tight square, ten by ten, apparently waiting for an order from their commander, the mounted knight, whose horse had long, slender horns growing out and upwards from either side of its skull.

'Where the hell are we?' whispered Flora, drawing the jacket closer around her body. She felt thinned, somehow, as if a vital part of her had been removed, and she was hungry. The smell of the jacket brought the image of Johnny vividly back to her, gangly and cool, lying on his bed with its Union Jack duvet, reading philosophy books and smoking.

'Not hell, I hope,' said Simon. 'Too cold for that.' The cool breeze rustled his hair.

'And no devils,' said Flora, looking at the knight's horse.

'Yet,' said Simon, under his breath.

Another procession, this one of riders, was coming from the city, apparently to join the soldiers. Only the cart was heading towards the city.

'We'd better keep out of sight,' Simon said. 'We don't know who we can trust. How can we get to the Broken King? Those soldiers might do anything to us. And we can hardly march up to them and demand to be taken to him, can we?'

'We have completed the tasks,' said Flora. 'That's what the messengers said. Complete the tasks, and get your siblings back.'

'I don't think it will be that easy . . .' said Simon.

Only a few days before, at home by the sea, he'd said the rhyme that had started it all, and it now rose unbidden in his mind:

I call the Broken King
Walk backwards thrice in a ring

He felt deeply afraid and pressed his forehead into the rock. He remembered his sister Anna being annoying. He'd said the rhyme to frighten her, and she'd been stolen away to this land. He remembered the golden messenger on the winged deer – the bird-deer, he'd called the beautiful, delicate creature – who'd appeared and told them what to do to rescue Anna and Johnny.

To get your siblings back, you must eat the shadow, steal the sun, and break the air . . .

And we did those three tasks, Simon thought, *to reach the Broken Kingdom. We ate the shadow, and got the shadow-spheres. We stole the sun, and gained the sunsword. We broke the air with the hunting horn. And that brought us here.*

Simon raised himself from the stone.

We are only at the beginning, he thought. He sensed a long road stretching out in front of him, through thick fog, never-ending. Suddenly overwhelmed with fear, and by the thought that they might never return home – and still less find their siblings – he clasped his hands over his head. What could they do? They had no plan, no idea where to go.

Flora slumped beside him. 'What about that knight who was after us – Sir Mark, the Knight of the Swan? Did he follow us in?'

'I hope he's not here . . .' said Simon, remembering the Broken King's sinister helper. Once more he peered carefully over the edge of the rocks. There was a swan swimming on the stream, and Simon watched it warily, recalling how Sir Mark had attacked him in that guise in his kitchen at home. The swan simply paddled away, and Simon, thinking of the knight's cruel face, couldn't help but feel relieved.

The cart was coming nearer to them, and Simon could now see that it was pulled slowly by a horse that had horns like a ram on both sides of its head, and a wide, heavy, black and white body. With gentle weariness, it blew air through its nostrils and shook its mane. A hooded man was hunched over on the cart's driving seat, his hands lightly on the reins. Sometimes he would swat the horned horse with a small whip, but the beast didn't move any faster.

As the cart trundled past them on the road, Simon

felt in his pocket and pulled out Hover, the little golden bird-deer he'd been given by the messengers. Hover was inert and drained of its golden sheen. It looked like a silver ornament of the kind Simon's granny kept on her mantelpiece.

'Is he moving? Is he telling you we can trust that carter?' Flora's breath was coming deep and fast.

Simon shook his head. 'Maybe things from the Golden Realm don't work in this world.'

Simon wished Hover would come alive again. He stroked its folded wings, and kissed its nose. Then he pressed it to the welt on his cheek where the golden messenger had struck on that first day by the sea.

Was it his imagination, or did the little creature stir slightly? He waited a second, but nothing further happened, so Simon put Hover back into his pocket.

Flora's head was between her knees, and Simon shifted and bent towards her and whispered her name.

Blinking, Flora looked up, and gulped back her tears.

'Are you all right?' asked Simon.

'I just . . . It's true! All this time I kept thinking maybe it was some kind of dream . . . even when we were running away from the Knight of the Swan

– but look, we're here! I'm not sure I can take it in properly . . .'

'It's OK,' he said, though he didn't feel it. 'We're almost there. That city – it must be the Broken King's city. Don't you recognise it from the book?'

Flora nodded. 'Have a look at the map.'

Simon found the skin-map, and Flora huddled next to him. 'There must be walls between the worlds,' she went on, jabbering slightly to cover up her nervousness, 'and somehow the sunsword and the hunting horn and the shadow-sphere all together make a split . . . I wonder how it works, physically? Light, sound and darkness . . . The walls came tumbling down . . . You see? Like Jericho.'

Simon smoothed out the skin-map on the rough ground. There was a green circle on the left. 'That must be where we've come from. I guess we'll have to get back here to reach home. Look!' He pointed to the standing stone near them. 'That must be the connection point between the worlds. And this,' he continued, indicating a line on the map, 'must represent the road leading to the city.' The city was on the right-hand side of the map. In its centre was a black dot, pulsing. 'And that's where they are.' Simon felt excitement bubble through him. 'We're there!'

'Almost,' said Flora. 'Now,' she continued in a more business-like tone, 'how are we going to get to the city? And what about Pike?' He was lying there, head at a slight angle, looking as if he'd been knocked out.

'Let's do a recce first,' said Simon. 'And then we'll try to wake him up again.'

They both peered over the rocks. On the broad, black plain in front of them, the mounted knight was addressing the band of soldiers.

The silver sun had moved higher up into the sky; the shadows had shortened. Axes and blades glinted in the silver light. They heard the mounted knight's orders.

'Attack the earth! Attack the trees! The king commands it!'

The soldiers split up. One half of them ran shouting towards a small scraggy copse. The trees had dark, purplish leaves and black bark. The other half began running in a circle, making swipes at the ground with their swords.

'What are they doing?' said Flora.

Waving their swords in the air, looking for all the world as if they were charging, the first group reached the trees and started hacking at the trunks, splitting the bark.

Meanwhile, the second group of soldiers was slashing at the turf, filling the sky with cries as if they were engaged with a deadly foe.

Across the plain, the column of riders on horned horses from the city was advancing nearer, mounted in six pairs and adorned in black and silver clothes and trappings, with a lone rider in green behind them. Following the rider was a litter draped with fine silver material, carried by eight tall men all dressed in white, and behind it came more riders, all bearing deadly weapons.

The mounted knight barked his orders with new urgency. Simon gripped Flora's arm. With a clattering of hooves and a swish of horse tails, the procession arrived beside the mounted knight, and came to a halt about twenty paces away from Flora and Simon.

The green rider, a willowy woman, theatrically pulled back the covering of the litter.

'Thank you, Andaria,' came a female voice, carried on the breeze. Inside the litter was a familiar young woman, wearing a glittering silver tiara and a long, black and silver gown. Her hands, also shining with gems, were clasped in her lap, and she raised one of them imperiously whilst Andaria helped her down.

'It's her!' exclaimed Flora. 'The girl in the lion mask! What's she doing here?'

'I thought she was dead!' said Simon.

'You thought Mithras killed her? That doesn't sound right. I don't think Mithras would kill anyone.' They'd left the lion-masked girl underneath the church in Walbrook Street in London, flat out on the ground after they'd fought her for the sunsword. That had been the last they'd seen of her. Mithras of the Golden Realm had been bending over her, apparently about to kill her.

The mounted knight waited nervously for some instruction from the girl. As the soldiers continued to run and hack, the young woman said, 'The king has given his order. And what he said is right.' Her voice was strong and rang out across the plain.

'And what he said is right!' came an answering chorus from the soldiers and the mounted knight.

The girl spoke again. 'I, Selena, the Silver Princess, daughter of the Ruler of the Silver Kingdom, deliver this his royal edict to his captain of arms, the Knight of the Hawk. The earth and the trees have been conquered. This unit is to take all spoils of war to the treasury. The battle has been won!'

'She's the *daughter* of the king?' whispered Flora to

Simon in a shocked undertone. 'The girl we fought? The girl we almost killed?'

'Revel in your conquest! The bards will sing of your prowess!' Selena motioned to Andaria, who hurled some coins on to the ground carelessly, as if they meant nothing to her. She might have spat, for all the expression of generosity on her face. 'A hundred crescents for the men!'

The Knight of the Hawk signalled to a soldier, who bent down and picked them up. The others watched him hungrily, but all waited.

Selena nodded, held out her arms, and two of her bearers lifted her gently back into the litter. Andaria, the green rider, pulled the curtains of the litter back across, and smacked one of the bearers out of her way with the flat of her hand, before remounting her snorting steed and leading the procession back to the city. They moved off, trappings jingling, and the Knight of the Hawk bit his lip, his horse whinnying, and a bead of sweat rolled down his cheek. He visibly relaxed, before straightening almost immediately and shouting out, 'At the ready!'

'Well . . .' said Flora, as the soldiers began to gather into a marching formation. 'That doesn't look like it was a . . . normal army thing.'

Simon didn't reply, but lifted a finger in warning.

'What?' said Flora, raising her eyebrows. 'Have I got something on my face?' She rubbed at her cheek, which only served to make it dirtier.

Simon pointed behind her.

Standing there was the hooded driver of the cart, holding a long, bright dagger. He'd noticed them as he'd driven past. His cart was pulled up a little way away from them. He stepped forwards and drew back his hood to reveal silver hair and a lined, tired face, his mouth twisted into a curiously off-putting smile. There was a tattoo on his neck, spidery and long. He was wearing a loose, brown tunic to his knees, and baggy cloth trousers.

He flourished the dagger casually at Simon and Flora. 'What are two bratlings doing outside the walls of the city? Show us your permit.'

'We . . . we lost it,' said Flora, as innocently as she was able, glad he hadn't seen Pike.

A white-eyed bird soared by, casting its shadow on the plain. In the distance they heard the soldiers marching back up the road to the city. They'd struck up a chant in time to their feet beating on the ground.

The carter came nearer, his expression now severe and glittering with calculation. 'Anyone found on the road without a permit is to be brought in. For fifty crescents' reward.'

'And then what?' said Simon.

'And then,' said the man, 'hurled in deepest, darkest prison, gnawed at by rats, and swung from the neck till they are no more.' He described the shape of a noose around his own neck with his left index finger. His gaze hardened. 'If you'd heard the decree, you would know.'

Flora gripped the sunsword's handle. But should she bring it out now? She was not sure. She inched it out of the sheath. As ever, she felt the warmth of its energy and a gentle hum in her mind, as if it were whispering to her somehow.

The carter, noticing the movement, grabbed Simon by the shoulder and held his dagger at his throat. Simon tried to wriggle free, but the man was strong.

Flora thought quickly. The carter was big, and he might kill Simon. But there was also the chance that he might lead them somewhere useful. A small chance, but a chance nonetheless. She pushed the sunsword back into its sheath. Perhaps they should go along with him, for now. He might even be able to gain them an audience with the Broken King, or know how to get to him. Pike would wake up and he might be able to find them later. She considered leaving a sign of some sort, glancing around covertly for anything she might use.

The carter took in Flora's leather jacket, and then her backpack. He winked leeringly at her, which made her shiver inside. 'You two are interesting. You look soft. Strange clothing. Palace bred, no doubt. So maybe you're rebels. Children of rebels, I'm thinking.' He snapped his finger, decisively. 'You're going to come with me.' He pushed Simon onwards, and Flora, biting the inside of her cheek, followed warily.

'You hurt him and it'll be the last of you,' she snapped.

The carter snorted disapprovingly, and as if to prove his point, stuck the tip of his dagger into Simon's arm. Simon yelped with the sharp pain.

'You leave him alone!' said Flora heatedly.

The carter swung round suddenly. 'Fifty crescents alive or dead,' he said. 'And what are you going to do about it, little girl? You show me.' He pushed Simon again, and Flora ran to keep up.

Chapter Two

CONCERNING
PIKE

FLORA'S ANGER AND sense of dislocation got the better of her and she began to argue with the carter. Her voice reached into Pike's mind where he lay by the stone, and prompted him to wake up with a start. Unsteadily, he got to his feet. Something was happening, nearby. Someone was in trouble.

Pike recognised the girl's voice through the roaring confusion of his consciousness. He saw Flora and Simon with the carter, and recognised his friends with a jolt. Without thinking, he crept forwards as quietly as he could. Then a terrible sickness took hold of him, seeping deep into his stomach and making his whole body shudder, and he had to stop to vomit on to the stony ground.

When he'd recovered, he wiped away the vile-tasting bile, and looked up to see that the carter was now leading Simon in a headlock, and Flora, helpless and drooping, followed beside him.

Something was tugging at his brain. He felt as if he was on the verge of an abyss. He searched for his knife, which was still in the pocket of his trousers. The texture of the clothing seemed wrong somehow. A bird's low booming made him look up, and the sound reminded him of something forcefully.

Fragments came into his memory; so many and so fast that they were almost overwhelming.

Flora began to shout, to beat her fists on the carter. Simon scrambled away from him, and the carter, surprised, knocked him to the ground. Simon landed on his back, spread-eagled. Flora jumped at the carter, and he reached for his dagger.

Pike remembered. The silver sun. A magehawk booming when warmth returns at the Festival of the Coming Rains. Something good flowed through him as the pale sunlight caressed his limbs. The fragments in his mind began to come together.

Simon was on his feet once more, lifting the hunting

horn from his neck, and holding it in front of him as a shield, just as the carter swiped his long knife. It bounced off, ringing. The carter took a step back.

Simon put the horn to his lips. The carter looked at it strangely.

He musn't blow it, thought Pike suddenly. And without thinking further, he ran, shouting, just as Simon blew. The vibrations bounced in his ears and the dust flew up underneath him as he went, hoping he could prevent the worst.

Something fell to the ground with a sickening thump. The carter's horned horse bellowed, more like a cow than anything else.

Pike reached Flora and Simon. The carter was lying on the earth, his silver hair spread out beneath him.

'Oh my God,' said Flora, her hand over her mouth on seeing Pike. 'And . . . oh my God! The carter! What happened to him?'

'Pike!' Simon looked very white and afraid.

The three of them embraced for a moment.

'I'm so glad you woke up . . .' said Flora.

'Ditto,' said Simon.

Pike felt a rush of tenderness, something he hadn't experienced for a long time. He released himself from their grasp, and they all three stood round the carter, looking down.

He was lying stretched out on his back, and he wasn't moving.

'Is he alive?' whispered Simon.

Flora bent down and touched the carter's tattooed neck, holding her finger there for a few seconds, before nodding. 'Just about.'

'I didn't mean to hurt him . . . I didn't know . . . Was it this?' Simon said, looking at the horn. 'It was this, wasn't it? Take it away!' Simon felt a sudden horror of the hunting horn and thrust it at Pike. Pike looked at it for a long moment, and then refused it, pushing it gently back at Simon.

Simon let the horn hang back against his ribs. He was shivering. He pulled himself together.

'No time to talk now,' said Pike. 'We need to get on to this cart and head to the city. But first, let's deal with this man.' He'd never sounded so decisive before. The silver light gleamed off him.

The three of them hefted the carter up and carried him off the road, leaving him hidden behind a rock. After pausing for a moment, Pike took the carter's trousers and top, and put them on. He left the carter a sack for warmth.

'What will happen to him?' asked Simon, worried, as they came back to the cart.

'He'll be all right,' answered Pike, getting into the driver's seat. 'He'll wake up soon enough. The only problem is that he might tell someone about you two. He doesn't know who you are, which is good, but the hunting horn – that's distinctive, and he might have heard stories about it. And then there's the odd way you two are dressed. It could raise suspicion. We'll have to hope he won't remember, or that he's too embarrassed about what happened, and he'll just slink home to his village with some story about bandits.' Pike set the horned horse moving. 'If anyone approaches, you two duck down,' he said.

'Firstly, though,' said Simon, 'thanks for rescuing us. Er, again.'

Pike blushed.

'But secondly,' continued Simon, 'you have a lot of explaining to do!'

'Yes,' said Flora. 'And you can start by saying where you're taking us! And how you know so much . . .'

Pike's face was grim. With a flick of the reins, he set the cart in motion towards the black towers that glittered ahead. 'You'll find out soon enough.'

Chapter Three

Towards
the City

PIKE WAS SNIFFING the air deeply. The broken
pictures in his mind were coming together. More
and more information became clear to him. He was
beginning to remember fully. Flora and Simon. He
had to bring them to the city. Why . . . he wasn't sure.
But there was something . . . It would come to him.
But above all they musn't be seen.

'Breathe in,' said Pike. 'That scent . . . the dew . . .
Fresh as the mornings when I used to . . .' And then it
was as if a gate had been unlocked in his mind, and a
flood of memories poured through.

'What is it, Pike?' asked Flora.

'I . . . used to ride here . . .'

'What are you saying?' said Simon. 'You've been here before?'

'On the dark plain outside the city, back when . . .' And the thought of his father came to him. The cart that had taken his father away. With a shock so bright it almost dazzled him, he remembered his father, encased in his silver armour, holding Pike's sword arm and showing him how to parry.

My father . . . No longer . . . My mother . . . The warmth of her eyes, her light. Now, exiled . . . He gasped with the force of it.

My mother is exiled, and my father is dead.

No, not just dead. Taken Apart.

The memory shook him for a second. He halted the cart, and steadied himself on the side. He remembered more. The meeting in the secret chamber in the ruined temple cave. The mission the princess had given him.

My mission. I've almost completed it, he thought.

He ignored Simon and Flora, their questioning voices seeming to come from far away. He tested his hands, stretched them, pinched different parts of himself, to see if he was dreaming.

I'm not dreaming. I'm here, he thought. *I'm . . .* And

he shaped the word 'home' in his mind, and a fierce joy filled his heart.

'Simon Goldhawk and Flora Williamson,' he said. He formed the syllables and tasted them on his tongue. He said the names as if he'd never said them before. How foreign and strange they sounded!

'Yes?' said Flora, uncertainly.

The two from the other world, from the place in-between. Though they called it the Earth. He, Pike, had been sent to help them come to the land of the Broken King.

Yes. That was it. He'd been ordered by Selena, the Silver Princess, the daughter of the king, who was working at great risk with an underground network to overthrow her father.

Yes. He remembered now. She sent him. To that other world . . . How odd it had been! That building where they'd found the shadow-spheres, all glass and brick, with all that strange food in it . . . And those machines that belched smoke and moved so fast, which you rode in . . . He sighed with the wonder of it.

He coughed and steadied himself. He had hardly any energy. The journey from the other world had taken it out of him. He had to tell the others.

'I am Pike!' he said. He faced Simon and Flora, and courage began to course through his veins. 'I am Pike! I am the son of the murdered Knight of the Shark and the exiled Lady of the Snake. I was sent to bring the ones . . .'

The urgency of it rushed through him and he all but stood up with excitement.

'I was sent to bring the ones who will topple the Broken King!'

The other two were silent, staring at him blankly. 'How can we trust you?' said Flora. 'I know! The bird-deer!'

'It doesn't work here,' said Simon.

'I have to take you to her . . . I have to bring you to the secret chamber in the temple cave, and send sign of this by magehawk.' *An arrow through a pair of horns*, he remembered. *But not on anything metal, nothing that doesn't come from something alive can be sent to her at the palace or it will be discovered.*

He would have to take them to the Silver Princess without getting discovered, as quickly as possible.

'Pike!' said Simon bluntly. In the silver light he thought Pike looked somehow more . . . right. He was taller, and the features of his face were more defined, chiselled even. He was almost handsome. He seemed like a completely different person. 'Who are you?'

After thinking for a moment, Pike spoke more calmly. 'My name is Pike. My father was the Knight of the Shark. He was Taken Apart by the Broken King, and my mother, the Lady of the Snake, was exiled.'

'So you're one of them?' said Flora nervously. 'You're from this world?'

'Yes. My memories are . . . fuzzy. The princess asked me to help you,' said Pike. 'The renegade princess. But she got rid of every memory in my mind, except the orders to aid you. She wanted to make sure that I didn't give myself away to the Knight of the Swan, or to any of his helpers. We cannot trust anybody. Now I'm back, everything is returning. I remember that the Knight of the Swan and my father, the Knight of the Shark, were once . . . allies.' His voice cracked a little. 'The Knight of the Swan is very persuasive. And who's to say that his persuasion would not have worked on me . . . But she – the princess – made it so that he would not recognise me, and I would not recognise him.'

'I don't like this . . .' said Flora quietly. 'You're telling us your father was an ally of our enemy . . . You're not telling us where you're taking us . . . I hardly recognise you!'

'What did your father do to be Taken Apart?' asked Simon.

Pike clamped his teeth together and urged the horned horse onwards.

'Don't!' said Flora. 'Don't move until you've explained!'

'I'm your friend,' said Pike fiercely. 'My father was one of the greatest knights this world has seen. He was the king's steward for a while. He did some . . . terrible things. And sometimes I hated him. But people did such things to protect themselves or their families. But in the end . . .'

'You mean he was on the Broken King's side?' exclaimed Simon.

'There is taking his side, or there is death.'

'Hang on,' said Simon, trying to suppress the tremor in his voice. 'You've just told us your father was *on his side*?'

Flora raised herself, eyes shining. 'Not you, Pike,' she whispered. 'Please, not you!'

'Not me,' said Pike gently. 'My mother . . . She's from the Golden Realm. She's one of Mithras's supporters. The snake –' He paused and gulped. 'There's someone coming. Duck!'

Flora and Simon dived down beneath some

sacking amongst the pungent root vegetables the carter had been carrying. Simon peered through the gaps in the side planking and saw a rider racing away from the city, drawing by close enough for him to make out that it was a woman dressed in green, before storming past.

'Listen,' Flora whispered to Simon, 'I'm not sure about all this. But let's watch him. We've got our weapons. And we can always escape if we need to. Just don't say anything for now. Deal?'

'Deal,' said Simon.

Chapter Four

THE

BLINDINGS

WHEN PIKE GAVE the all clear, Simon and
Flora sat back up. A shimmering cloud of
dust was all that remained of the rider. 'She's going to
the port of Notus,' said Pike. 'There must be trouble
down there.'

'Who is it?' asked Flora.

Pike sniffed. 'Andaria. Best to avoid her.'

Ahead of them, the soldiers were almost at the
gates, which were painted with huge silver eyes that
glared out across the plain. The city loomed, cold
and grim, and Simon's heart quailed. Simon watched
as the great gates slid open smoothly, creating a

view into the city. He glimpsed flags and banners fluttering in the breeze and people rushing about, before the soldiers went through and the gates closed firmly behind them.

'She's not the princess?'

'No. You met the princess already,' said Pike, answering Simon's question. 'She was the girl in the lion mask.'

'And,' continued Pike, 'my guess is when she last saw you that she didn't fight you very hard.'

'You mean she wanted us to win and get the sunsword? She let us win?' said Flora slowly. 'She was working against her father . . .'

'That is exactly what she did. She's Selena, a daughter of the king, known as the Silver Princess. She's been secretly allied with the rebels for the last few years. They plan to overthrow the king and put her in his place. She plotted with Mithras so that you would gain the sunsword, and he would be set free.'

'What do you think?' whispered Simon to Flora. 'I think he's all right, don't you?'

Flora nodded, and spun the sunsword over in her hands, glad she hadn't yet used it in battle. *But I want to*, another voice whispered in her head, and she wondered if it was the sunsword speaking to her. 'Don't be silly,' she said to herself, before turning back to Simon.

A cloud scudded past the silver sun, sending shadows racing across the plains on either side of them, rolling towards the hills. They passed some burned-out husks of houses where nothing but rats scratched in the remains.

'When we get to Selena, you'll learn everything. It's not safe to talk out here,' said Pike.

The gates ahead were tall and iron, studded with cruel-looking bolts. The painted eyes disconcerted them. Soldiers ranged along the top of the walls facing out in all directions. Two guards in full metal body armour stood on either side of the gates, each holding a halberd, and each with a sword hanging from his belt. The guards looked thin, and there was hunger in their eyes.

'How will we get through?' said Simon.

'I'll think of something . . .' said Pike. 'Now, stay down.' He turned round in his seat.

Flora and Simon crouched back beneath the sacking.

'Simon?' whispered Flora, as the cart came to a creaking stop and the horned horse stamped its front hoof and whisked its tail. One of the guards clanked forwards to talk to Pike.

'What?'

'I was just wondering . . .' She gulped. 'I was just wondering . . . How . . . ? I mean, we never – we never asked how we were going to get back.'

Simon didn't reply. But he had the same feeling of uncertainty, deep in his heart. They were being led by a son of a servant of the Broken King into the king's own city. Had they been mad to trust Pike? Perhaps they should get away from him, as soon as possible.

But then . . . Pike had saved them, and said he was taking them to the princess – to someone working against the king. Surely she would help them rescue the prisoners?

But were they doomed to stay here for ever? If they did succeed, would they come back to their own world and find it changed beyond measure? Images of deserted streets and ruined houses entered his mind. He saw his parents' cottage by the sea as it was when he'd left it, and then he watched it crumble into dust. *And if we fail, then it will be as if we'd never existed . . .*

No, he thought. *Don't even imagine it.*

He pictured his parents lying in the golden, charmed sleep the messengers had put them in, hidden in another fold of reality, out of reach of the world that he and they knew, existing outside of time. He felt a tug of sadness.

Pike was speaking in an accent like the carter's to one of the guards, asking for passage into the city.

'What have you got in there?' said the guard.

Through the slats Simon could see chain mail and a sword held by thick, square-tipped fingers.

'Roots,' muttered Pike.

'Why're you coming in now? Market's not till later.'

The other guard paced to the side of the cart and looked in. 'Orders of the king – we search every cart that comes in.'

Simon held his breath. Flora made herself very small.

Pike improvised. 'Was on way back home when little brother came and met me, yelling – old mother Jana's got the black spot. Came back straight. Got to get some herbs for old mother.'

The guard poked about amongst the roots. His mailed hand appeared right in front of Simon's nose, so close he could see the dirt encrusted under the nails.

'You touch that boy?' said the guard.

'No,' said Pike. 'Turned back, came here straight. Didn't touch him, didn't go near him.'

'You got a lot of roots here,' said the guard, after a pause. 'How many do you reckon you have?'

Pike swallowed, thinking fast. The guard was picking up one of the roots, and sniffing at it. 'More'n enough,' said Pike.

'More'n enough. So, a couple of sacks fell off your cart, didn't they?' said the guard nonchalantly.

Before Pike could say anything, the other guard stepped forwards and hefted off two sacks from the cart. Simon and Flora tensed, but the sacking covering them remained in place.

The first guard flicked the root he was holding up into the air, caught it, then threw it back at Pike. It hit him on the chest and fell to the ground.

'Get in with you,' said the guard. 'Get your herbs, and get out before sundown. Listen out for the new decrees. Come through, and be lucky.'

Pike released his breath. 'Be lucky,' he said. The chains of the gate clanked, and he moved the cart on. The horned horse snorted and stamped through the gates, which slammed shut behind them.

After a while, Pike said, 'You can come out now.'

Simon and Flora gingerly poked their heads out. They were going along a narrow street between thin wooden houses that clustered together and leaned into one another. They looked small, grimy and dark; scraps of rags fluttered at the windows, and shutters hung off hinges. A woman was scratching about in the gutter, poking at piles of rubbish. And yet the road's surface glittered and shone, made from a substance that they did not recognise. As the houses were not high, they could see the two towers on the hill rising ahead, looming over all below them.

Outside every couple of houses hung a portrait. Some were huge – bigger than a person. Others were smaller. But they all showed the same face: a man with a blank gaze, white face, thin red lips and black eyes. Horns came out from the sides of his head, curving upwards, and he was wearing a golden crown.

The king, guessed Simon, and shuddered. *Can he see us? Can those eyes see us?* He pushed the disquieting thought away.

People were walking along the street quickly, heads down, some forlornly clutching sacks that didn't look very full, others holding fluttering birds in cages, or leading thin, horned beasts that looked a little like goats. They wore drab, shapeless clothes, much like the carter's. Nobody was talking, and nobody was laughing. The near-silence was eerie. Their eyes gleamed when they saw the roots on the cart, but Pike didn't stop, and nobody tried to steal from them.

'We'll hide the cart and the horse somewhere close by. They might come in useful. And then I'll take you on foot to . . . her . . .' said Pike, leaning over. 'We'll have to be extremely careful. I'll have to do something about your clothes.'

Simon looked down at his blue jeans, which did appear strange even to his own eyes, set against the cart and sacking. Flora smelled the leather jacket and inhaled deeply.

'I like my trainers,' said Flora, mock-sulkily. 'And this is one of my favourite skirts . . .'

Pike's knowledge of the city was coming back to him, burning brightly in his mind. They'd come in through the main gate, which faced out towards Notus, named for the south wind. The gate opened into a residential district called the Blindings, through which they were now going.

Further in the direction of Boreas, the north wind, below the palace hill, was the central square of the first ruler of the Kingdom, King Silvanus the

Magnificent. Around the square were gathered the vast houses and towers of the knights, where Pike had spent much of his life before his father had been Taken Apart. And on the northern side, on top of the hill, was the palace of King Selenus, the mad, the broken.

Pike turned his thoughts back to where they could put the cart and horse. Around the corner, further into the Blindings, was a network of narrow streets and alleys where he could hide them. He'd tie up the horned horse and have to hope that nobody stole her – or worse, took her for meat. He pulled her to a halt down a quiet, dark little street, and got down on to the cobbles, patting the horned horse on the flank, and then pulling some old bits of cloth over the sacks of roots. They too might be a temptation, and he didn't want to draw attention to the stolen cart. He looked at Simon and Flora critically. 'You can cover yourselves with sacking,' he said. 'It'll have to do for the moment.

'Why can't we use the shadow-spheres?' said Simon.

'You've only got two left each,' said Pike. 'Two for you both and your siblings. So you shouldn't use them unless you have to. They don't really make you invisible, either. It's more about . . . realigning things. They don't last between worlds.'

'How did you get through without one?' asked Flora.

Pike looked surprised. 'You had to do the tasks as the king set them to get here. I live here. It's easier for people to get back to their own world. I just followed you in. But without a portal like that, it's harder. One way for us is through our animals, though not everyone can do it – you have to develop the skill. The Knight of the Swan uses his swans on your side. It's difficult, though. Then there are the holding places, which bubble up between the worlds – Mithras was kept in one, and the ambassadors you met – Raven, Cautes and Cautopates.'

Flora turned out the contents of one of the sacks, tore a hole in it with Pike's knife, and then did another one for Simon.

'Ready?' said Pike. 'Let's –'

He was interrupted by a loud, insistent tolling of bells. His face paled. 'Oh no . . . that's coming from the king's palace.'

'What does it mean?' asked Simon.

'It means the king is about to issue a new decree.'

They quickly emptied the items from the rucksack

into another sack. Though the tent was too big to take, they kept the skin-map, two bottles of water, the porcupine spine that Anna had given Simon, the button, Johnny's syringe, the pencil stub and the torch.

'This'll work here, right?' said Simon, flicking the torch switch. It did.

Flora wrapped the sheathed sunsword in another piece of sacking, and fitted it into her belt, concealing it with the shapelessness of the sack she was wearing over the top. Simon hid the hunting horn under his arm, and felt it strange, lying against his skin.

The bells continued to ring into the air, and men and women came hurrying from out of the houses.

'Hurry now! Carry a bag of roots over your shoulder and nobody will notice you. We'll just keep quiet till we get there. If anyone stops us – anyone at all – let me do the talking.'

'How far is it?' asked Flora.

'Not far.'

Everyone was moving in the same direction. Pike cursed. 'That's annoying. We're more likely to be noticed now.'

A tall, silver-haired woman rushed closely past them. She was very thin, and her cheeks were hollow. She caught Simon's eye as she sped by. 'Why aren't you hurrying to hear the decree of our benevolent king Selenus?'

'Come on,' said Pike, picking up a sack. 'We've got to go now, or it'll look even more suspicious.'

Simon hefted a sack of roots over his shoulder, and Flora took the other sack with their few possessions in it, and they all set off.

Pike led them into the hastening throng. Everyone was looking down, but they were all glancing nervously at each other as well. Some younger men and women wore striking tunics embroidered with animal symbols – a hare, a boar, and some other beasts that were strange to Simon and Flora. These people were given space; as if by magic, a clear path would form in front of and behind them. Knights in armour – some black, some in reds, greens and blues – strode smartly, some carrying their helmets. The crowd carefully avoided the knights, and the knights took no apparent notice of the crowd.

'Keep close behind,' whispered Pike.

They pressed on through the crowds, the angry ringing of the bells filling the air.

Chapter Five

THE KING
DANCES

S IMON WAS RUSHING along the city streets, keeping his eyes firmly fixed on Pike. Pike's brown clothing, taken from the carter, was so similar to almost everyone else's that Simon didn't want to lose sight of him for a second. The sack of roots was heavy, and his shoulder was getting sore. Flora was keeping pace with Simon, the sunsword bumping into her leg. She ignored it. They walked quickly for maybe ten minutes. *Do they even call them minutes here?* thought Simon, madly.

Sometimes the shadowy black birds with their white eyes would swoop low overhead, calling their deep cries.

'Magehawks,' said Pike in answer to Simon's enquiring glance. 'They take messages. Extremely clever, and they can use the shadows to travel over long distances.'

More and more people came pouring out of alleys, appearing from the doors of houses and crowding out of other tall buildings, all streaming one way. It was, guessed Simon, about two and a half hours since they'd arrived in this strange, other world. Hunger stretched his belly, and thirst parched his throat and lips, but he didn't seem to feel it as keenly as he would at home.

There wasn't much time to take in their surroundings, but Simon tried to keep a sense of the direction in which they were going. He felt the sun, warm on the back of his neck, about a quarter of the way up the sky, and he attempted to orient himself from where they'd come. Soon, though, he was confused, as they went down winding roads and the wooden houses gave way to brick and glass, and then back to wooden. He began to feel that they were walking in circles.

They passed along streets paved with black cobbles. They were jostled and shoved, and they tried to look as inconspicuous as possible, especially so whenever an armoured knight or a soldier marched past. Once or twice a proud horned horse with a rider would trot through the crowds; sometimes soldiers, shifty-looking and clasping weapons, made their way by, stepping past to a chant.

Soon, they came out into a wider avenue lined with tall lampposts, trees and with soaring black glass buildings on either side. Each lamppost was carrying its own portrait of the King. *This street is like the one in my vision*, thought Simon, and shivered. He remembered how he'd seen Anna, crouching in the corner of a dark room. *I hope she's all right.*

Music was coming from somewhere, wild and haunting, and it made the hairs stand up all along Simon's arms. The dark foliage of the trees was dotted with buds, and from the branches were hanging what looked like rolled-up parchments, but which Simon knew from experience were sure to be the remains of the dead.

'We're almost there,' said Pike. The street they were on led into a huge square. In the centre was a large bronze statue of a crowned man with horns on either side of his head. He was mounted on a horned horse, which looked fierce and huge, nostrils flaring, muscles rippling. The statue held a sword above his head. 'That's not Selenus. It's our first king,' said Pike, following Simon's questioning look. 'Silvanus the Magnificent. Centuries ago. Let's wait here.'

He dragged Simon and Flora to a place where they could stand on a slightly raised stone platform, set back from the main square, and away from the hustling crowd. 'That's the king's palace,' whispered Pike, pointing to a tall black building above them at the top of a small hill. Two towers rose on either side of a lower black colonnade, from which a couple of wings stretched out to form a courtyard. A slope led down from there to the level of the paving where the crowd was gathering. Above the palace fluttered three flags – two of which were a black and silver design; the central one was white with a pair of black horns on it. *Like the horns on the map*, thought Simon.

The square was filling with people. They were not noisy; there was only a quiet murmuring. The feeling was one of tension. Mounted guards stood along the palace side of the square, holding lances, helmets flashing.

Smaller towers were clustered near the palace. These had balconies on which stood men, women and children in much finer clothes than those around Simon. *Those must be the families of the knights*, he thought.

Many of the towers had flags and banners decorated with animal symbols – a lion, a dolphin, a butterfly, a horned horse – while others simply had colours. Some balconies were thronged; others were empty.

'That was mine,' whispered Pike, pointing to a tower on the right. Nobody stood on its balconies, though lights still glimmered from the windows. 'I do not know who lives there now . . . My father's people would have fled, like I did.'

The murmur of the crowd began to ebb away. A horn sounded, and Simon grabbed the handle of the one around his neck. It was humming with its own power, almost as if it were alive. *I wonder what else it can do?* he thought. *Would different gradations of sound have different effects? Could it kill someone?* Simon shivered. *I would not like to kill a man*, he thought, and hoped the carter was all right. He pinched hold of Flora's elbow, and she looked at him gratefully. 'Nice place to grow up,' she whispered into his ear. 'Though it beats Moreton in the Green . . .'

'London's more fun than this, though,' said Simon. He remembered how he'd hated Limerton when his family had moved there from London, after his dad lost his job. *And now what would I give to get back there*, he thought.

Doors opened in the base of the central wing of the palace, and out came two riders in black and silver. Behind them marched a pair of tall men dressed entirely in silver clothing, holding up a canopy. Underneath it walked Princess Selena, in close-fitting silver armour and with a sword belted at her waist.

She reached a podium. The crowd was entirely silent.

'The king has spoken,' said Selena, 'and what he said is right.'

All the people replied, 'And what he said is right.'

Pike mumbled it and nudged Simon and Flora, who quickly did the same.

The men in silver walked backwards away from Selena, lowering the canopy.

'People of the Kingdom!' Her voice echoed as she gazed out across the square. 'Today two agents of the Golden Realm entered the bounds of our kingdom. They are not of the Golden Realm, nor this our Silver Kingdom.'

Mutterings of fear and worry rose up from the crowd.

'They are from the world in-between.'

Pike started edging Flora and Simon gently

towards one of the square's exits. Others eagerly filled their places, eyes bent on Selena.

'Anybody found harbouring them or aiding them in any way will be imprisoned,' said Selena.

A voice rang out above the crowd. 'How will we know them?'

'They are a boy and a girl,' said Selena.

Pike breathed a sigh of relief. She hadn't mentioned him. She was protecting him, he realised. Quietly, he marshalled Flora and Simon towards a shadowy stone archway and paused there.

'And now,' said Selena, 'the king has ordered a Taking Apart.' Was it Simon's imagination, or was there a crack in her voice?

A shiver ran through the crowd, the people rustling and bending like a field of grass in the wind.

'Our lord chancellor, the Crimson Knight, has been found guilty of the highest treason.'

Shocked gasps pierced the air.

'The Crimson Knight,' said Pike quietly. 'I knew him. He gave me a dagger when I was young and lifted me up on to his shoulders to watch the Dance of the Sinking Moon. I played with his daughter. She had bright hair, and she beat me at wrestling. Scarlet, she was called.'

There was a small commotion, and two guards appeared from inside the palace. Walking between them was a man in bright red armour, wearing no helmet, his chin held high. He had no chains, though the guards held him by the elbows, and they made their way at a steady pace down the hill towards the podium where the princess stood. He was followed by a man wearing a black and silver mask, who carried a mallet, and led four horned horses.

'The Crimson Knight,' read Princess Selena from a scroll. 'Sir Jacobus, the twelfth of his rank, fourth chancellor since the blessed reign of our father began. You have been lord chancellor for our king these past few months.'

Her hands are trembling, thought Simon.

'His High Majesty, the King Selenus, finds you, in his absolute wisdom, guilty of the highest treason. Your sentence: to be Taken Apart.'

The Crimson Knight's face twitched. Suddenly, he broke free of his captors, and strode to the podium. He was a tall man, fleshy-faced with white hair. Simon quite liked the look of him.

He just managed to shout out, 'Hear this!' as the guards leaped at him and restrained him. 'Our king is mad! There has been no trial. I am no traitor! I am accused and condemned for naught! What is my charge? Read out my charge . . .'

There was movement in the crowd now, like ripples in the surface of a lake. *They are all terrified*, thought Simon.

'The charge is one of the highest treason, sir knight,' said Princess Selena.

Guards flocked towards the Crimson Knight.

'Time to go,' said Pike, his voice tight and serious. 'You don't want to see this.'

'Wait!' said Flora. 'I want to see . . .'

'Me too,' said Simon.

A soldier stripped him of his armour and threw it clanging to the ground. He stood there, all but naked in a white shift, looking frail and vulnerable.

The man in the black and silver mask took the knight's sword, placed it on a stone, and swung at it with a huge mallet. It shattered, surprisingly, and the shards flew through the air like glass. The Crimson Knight made no noise, but he was obviously deeply distressed.

'Let's go,' said Pike. 'We're not watching this . . .' He steered them away from the scene.

As they departed, Simon looked over his shoulder and saw a space being made in the square.

One horned horse was being tied to each limb of the Crimson Knight, and as they turned a corner into a darker, cobbled street, the screams of the knight began over the deathly silence of the crowd.

Pike pushed them into the shadow of another archway on the southern side of the square, from where they could see the horses and part of the crowd. There was a small wall beside it, behind which they could be concealed; the arch gave, on the other side, on to a quiet street. They settled into the side of the arch.

The screams stopped, and the crowd remained still. Somebody was sobbing, but the sobbing ended as soon as it had begun.

Suddenly the crowd broke up. People rushed back to where they'd come from, eyes down, not speaking.

'Wait here.' Pike told them to crouch behind the sacks of roots, with the other bits of sacking draped over them, so that they could just see over the top of the wall but remain concealed. 'Hopefully nobody will notice you. Don't speak to anyone and don't draw attention to yourselves.'

We hardly need telling, thought Simon. He squashed up next to Flora. Pike vanished into the crowd, which was now flowing past in all directions.

After a while, Flora whispered, 'What if he doesn't come back? Or . . .'

Or worse, what if he comes back with someone else? Someone who won't help us . . . The thought had struck Simon, too. *And what if he's on the side of the Broken King? What if he's gone straight to him, and will catch us here, like flies in a spider's web, and make us his toys, just like Anna and Johnny?*

'You trust him, don't you?' asked Simon. 'We said we would . . . He's helped us so much . . .'

'I don't know what to think any more,' said Flora.

They looked out across the square, up towards the king's palace. Simon caught a glimpse of a wagon with something bloody and obscene in it, and supposed that it must contain the remains of the Crimson Knight. The lord chancellor, he'd been . . . and now he was nothing. The wagon stopped by a tree, and the people on it started to do something to the knight's body parts.

Flora was tapping her foot. 'Can't we explore just a little bit?' She was slowly returning to her old self. She rubbed at her eyes. 'What must I look like!'

Simon shook his head. 'I don't think so. They're all on the look-out for an odd boy and girl. We'd be hauled in immediately. Unless you want to chop your hair off and disguise yourself as a boy, of course.'

'Couldn't we find a wig and disguise you as a girl?' said Flora, poking Simon in the belly. 'You'd be good as one.'

Simon blushed deeply but couldn't think of anything to say in reply, so bit his tongue instead. He was finding it hard to place his feelings about Flora. He did not know what he would do if she were not there. She made him feel warm, but also heightened and dizzy. *Why is everything so complicated?* he thought, and sighed.

The square was emptying out. Soon people were going past in ones and twos, none greeting each other, none stopping to admire the statues or the buildings, all feeling the great eyes of the king's portraits upon them.

Something strange was happening to the Crimson Knight's remains. They were being rolled up – like the skin-map – and hung from the trees. Simon looked away.

A magehawk perched on a railing and tilted its head towards them. It was quite large and dark, and its edges were shadowy and blurry. Its eyes were white and shining.

'I'm sure it's looking at us,' whispered Simon.

'Don't be silly,' whispered Flora, who was starting to feel a bit stiff. 'Pike's been ages. Do you think it gets dark here? Do you think their day is as long as ours? Is that the sun?' She pointed at the silver orb, which was about halfway across the sky, presumably at its highest point.

The strange bird flapped its wings, squawked, and flew off. Simon relaxed.

And then a change came over the air. The few remaining in the square all paused and, as if obeying a signal, scurried away as quickly as possible. Simon sensed their fear and drew Flora closer to him.

There was a sound of chains being pulled, and the gates of the palace drew themselves open.

Out of them came two monkeys. Or at least, they looked like monkeys, capering about, dressed in little green and gold embroidered jackets and red trousers, but they didn't have tails. They were followed by a giant of a man in a long, white robe, holding hands with a very small woman dressed in black.

Behind them was a delicate horned horse, which was drawing a tiny, jewelled open carriage, round which eight guards were tightly packed, four on each side, all holding spears.

And in the carriage was a man, seated on a tall

blue velvet chair. His hair was entirely silver. That seemed to be the case with many of the people here, Simon realised. This man's hair was long, longer than the carter's, flowing down his shoulders, thin and bright. Stranger still was that he had horns growing on either side of his head, arching up almost to a point.

A growing sense of horror crept over Simon. *That's him*, he thought. *That's the Broken King. He's the one who took Anna.*

The king was surrounded by a dark, shifting substance. It was almost see-through – not quite like smoke, more like gauze, clinging to him like a garment. *Ectoplasm* was the word that came to Simon.

Behind the king was a larger carriage, also open to the air.

On it were two young people. Simon and Flora's hearts both began to beat a little faster.

'Don't!' Simon restrained Flora, who shifted beneath the sacking.

'But it looks like –' said Flora.

Simon nodded. *I know*, he thought.

The little procession was coming down the right-hand side of the square, and as it drew nearer, Simon's hopes were confirmed.

One of the pair on the carriage was a good-looking young man, maybe eighteen or so, thought Simon. There was something strange about him. Light glinted off his cheek, as if it had been carved out of silver, but the rest of him was normal.

Simon didn't need to look at Flora to know that it was Johnny. Flora gripped his hand, her face shining with anticipation. Johnny was leaning over the side of the carriage, gazing about keenly.

And joy and excitement began to pour through Simon as well. Next to Johnny, in a long, ridiculous red dress, and with a golden coronet on her head, was his little sister, Anna. She was holding her dress up to her body, as if it were a blanket. Her hands glinted silver, too, from where her skin had been taken to make the skin-map.

'Flora,' hissed Simon. 'What do we do?' Thoughts were rushing about his head. They could leap out, use the sunsword and the hunting horn, rescue their siblings . . . and then what?

The procession trundled around the square, along the side where Simon and Flora were hiding.

'They're coming here,' said Simon frantically. They drew the sacking over their heads, and crouched down lower. There was nothing between them and the paving but a low wall.

The monkeys were jumping about, and as they came nearer Simon saw with horror that they weren't monkeys at all, but odd, humanoid creatures with terrible grins. *Don't let those spot us*, he thought, shuddering.

As if reading his mind, one of the pair stopped and sniffed the air. Catching the smell of the roots, it bounded towards them, closely followed by its companion.

The two creatures entered the space beneath the black arch. Simon tensed. They were vile little things. One of them leered and bared its teeth, showing a mass of jagged, yellowed, broken ivory.

The nearer one advanced. Simon and Flora stayed as motionless as they could. The creature put out a paw – if you could call it a paw. It was a mangled thing, all twisted and scarred.

One squealed, and reached towards a sack.

Just as its companion pushed it out of the way to get a closer look, a command came from behind, and the creatures stiffened, looked at each other in alarm, and scampered back to their positions.

Flora and Simon relaxed.

As the jewelled carriage containing the king went past, his words came clear on the air.

'My people! My people! My people acclaim me!'

The gauzy shadowy substance around him shifted and flowed. A magehawk was perched on the back of the carriage, and it too was blurry at the edges. *They can use the shadows,* Simon thought. *Is that what's around the king? Some kind of shadow? A form of protection, perhaps . . .*

And then the carriage with Anna and Johnny went by. Anna's expression was hard to read. Her hands were held awkwardly. She was trying to hide the silver. She looked, in spite of her long dress and coronet, frightened.

Simon wanted to jump out and save her, rescue her right now, but the thought of what might happen to him at the hands of those two creatures, or on the points of the guards' weapons, prevented him, as did the notion of what the consequences to Anna might be. *I've harmed her enough already,* he thought, and the guilt that was always at the back of his mind burst forth and shrouded his brain for a second.

'Hear them rejoice!' called the king.

Simon studied Johnny – the young man was in a golden robe and he was also crowned with a circlet of gold. He was alert, looking about, keeping an eye on the guards.

Simon soon saw why. As the carriage turned to

go back up the other side of the square, Johnny took something from out of the folds of his robe. Simon couldn't see it very clearly, but it looked like a small dagger. Before Simon even had time to follow the movement, Johnny had thrown it at the king.

The dagger flew into the king's shadow. The shadow fizzed, briefly, and then the dagger fell to the ground, where it clattered and lay still. The guards shouted. The king did not move. Instead he grinned, savagely.

Johnny flung himself over the edge of the carriage. He landed neatly on the paving, and began to run.

Flora gasped and almost threw off the sacking, but Simon managed to restrain her. Luckily none of the procession noticed her, as the guards, the giant and the little creatures all began to chase after Johnny. The king remained where he was, his shadow swirling about him like a cloak in the wind.

Simon couldn't see where Johnny ran to, but could hear the sound of pursuit. A few seconds later there was a shout of triumph, and the giant and one of the guards dragged Johnny back between them – not too roughly, Simon noted.

'Well done, Bruin!' called the king. Then, more softly, 'You shouldn't have done that, my Johnny.'

'I wanted to hurt you!' shouted Johnny. The guard

punched him in the stomach, and he doubled over, then raised himself up again. 'Cowards!'

Simon looked towards Anna. She was gripping the edge of the carriage, staring at Johnny.

'Try again, Johnny. Try to hurt me,' taunted the king. 'You know it's not possible. Why do you hate me so much, Johnny?'

Johnny's shoulders sagged.

The giant, Bruin, loaded Johnny back on to the carriage. Anna flung herself at him, and Johnny kneeled to hug her.

Two guards lifted the Broken King down out of his carriage, and he was now pacing up and down, holding a hand cupped to his ear. It seemed he had already forgotten about Johnny. 'They sing for me! Hear them sing! The Crimson Knight is gone, and how they sing!'

He started to dance. From left to right, from right to left, and back again, he glided and swayed, all the time singing a haunting song that sounded like a folk melody Simon vaguely knew.

'Dance with me! Dance with me!' he shouted. Bruin the giant and the little woman held hands, and started to twirl about, Bruin lifting the woman off the ground solemnly. Neither of them smiled.

The two monkey creatures squawked and chattered and leaped; Johnny and Anna were dragged down from their carriage, and Simon and Flora watched with terrible unease as their siblings danced, tears streaming down their faces, around the Broken King.

Just as abruptly as it began, it stopped, and the king stood still, raised out his arms, and was carefully placed back into the carriage, where he took his seat on the blue velvet chair, smoothing down his robes and flashing a dark smile.

'The shadow abides,' he shouted. 'The shadow abides!' And then the driver of his carriage flicked his whip, the horned horses whinnied, and the king's carriage and the rest of the procession made their way along the other side of the square, up the slope of the hill, and through the gates of the palace. Then the palace gates slammed shut, leaving only a black, unbroken surface with the other buildings reflected in it.

Simon sat back, exhausted. Flora whistled through her teeth, and slumped down. Neither said anything more. They heard nothing but the occasional wheel on the ground, and once a distant argument.

It could have been any amount of time later that Pike's face appeared over the top of the wall.

'You two look tired,' he said. 'What did I miss?'

Chapter Six

THE LADY
OF THE STAG

SIMON WAS SCRATCHING his armpits. Flora
was looking similarly uncomfortable. After they'd
told Pike what they'd seen, he'd thrust some grey and
brown garments at them, made from a very coarse
cloth, and one pair each of some plain brown leather
slippers. They stuffed their old clothes and trainers in
with their other possessions inside one of the sacks.

Pike had found the horse and cart where he'd left
them, undisturbed, and had managed to sell the roots
to a chance passer-by – clearly for a good deal, as the
buyer had looked absolutely delighted and scuttled off
home, laden with sacks, as fast as he was able. With the

money, Pike had bought some clothes, and there were a few crescents left over that would serve them well.

With the garments on, Simon and Flora looked just like any other ordinary citizen in the Kingdom, except for Flora's make-up, now more smudged than ever.

'You'd better wash that off,' said Pike. 'Whatever it is.'

'Huh,' said Flora. 'It's called eyeliner.' But she dutifully splashed herself with freezing cold water until there was only the faintest outline of black left around her eyes. 'You two might like to think about using it some day. It can look good on boys too, you know. Guyliner, they call it.'

'I'm not a goth,' said Simon.

'Stop saying such strange things,' hissed Pike. 'Listen, I'm taking you to what you'd call the east of the city.'

'What do you call it?' said Flora.

'We call directions by the names of the four winds. So, Eurus. It's like the Blindings, but quieter.'

'The directions on the skin-map were marked by letters . . .' said Simon. 'For Boreas. Eurus . . . What was the N for?'

'Notus,' said Pike.

'And Zephyrus,' finished Flora. 'You have the

same winds as us. Or rather, the Romans.'

Pike looked surprised. 'Romans? I think I've heard of them . . . Something from my history tutor . . .' he said. 'They're in your world, aren't they? A long time ago . . . And there was something about them . . . Something to do with King Silvanus, I think . . . But I forget. I never paid much attention to my tutors – I was always too worried about everything else going on . . . We'll head to the meeting place. And then signal Selena, the Silver Princess. And after that . . .' He shuddered. 'War is coming. War, and the killing of a king.'

The streets around them as they headed east were far less imposing than those directly around the palace square. The buildings were two or three storeys high and made from brick, stone and wood. All had dark glass windows. The portraits of the king were ever-present.

Simon had a strange sense of not quite fitting in, as if he were a jigsaw piece from the wrong puzzle. *Like how Pike must have felt in our world,* he thought. *And now Pike looks so natural, so at home.*

As they walked down the narrowing streets, wooden houses became more common, two storeys high at most, with gabled roofs. A market was coming to an end along the centre of the road. Simon watched a fat, wheezing man haggling over the price of what looked very much like a chicken.

'What's that?' asked Simon, pointing at it as it clucked and flapped.

Pike looked blank for a second. 'That? Oh that's a – what d'you call it? A chicken.'

'Oh,' said Simon, winking at Flora. 'Does anyone get to be Knight of the Chicken?'

Pike looked serious. 'Not that I know of,' he said. 'I would check in the scrolls, if I could find some safely . . .' Flora and Simon giggled between themselves.

The silver sun was now slowly making its way towards the horizon, and the shadows were stretching out across the roads. Simon looked carefully at the stalls as they went by. Some of them had cages, in which were magehawks like the one he'd seen earlier. They hooted, deep and long.

His eye was caught by two little girls, playing with a dark animal, all black and fierce, like the royal hound that had attacked them in their own world. Simon instinctively shivered.

'Don't worry,' said Pike, guessing what he was thinking. 'That's just a normal hound. The royal ones are specially bred for ferocity.'

Indeed, the little hound was playful and was jumping at a piece of bone one of the girls was holding just out of its reach. The only strange thing about it was quite how black it was, as if it too were made of shadows. It growled a little, and the girl, shrieking, dropped the bone and caught her friend in mock horror.

The traders were packing up their stalls and sweeping away scraps from the day's business. Pike jingled the handful of coins he had left over from the sale of the roots. Simon had one of them in his pocket – it was large, like an old-fashioned two-pence piece he'd seen in his grandparents' house, but made from a silver metal, and it bore the profile of the king on one side, and on the other a crescent moon.

Flora was wondering about where exactly they were, and what the people around them were. Not elves, or anything like that. Although they looked human, they were definitely different. Like people in a dream. And what did that make her and Simon to them? They were from the world in-between . . . but in-between what?

She noticed a magehawk perched on top of a house. Its white eyes followed her. She nudged Pike and pointed.

Pike looked around, then ducked furtively into an alleyway. The magehawk fluttered to another vantage point. He beckoned to Simon and Flora, who then followed. The alleyway was only about the width of three people, and it ended in a brick wall.

'We're safe in here,' said Pike. Simon watched behind them, and sure enough the magehawk flew across the gap, but didn't come down the alley. It boomed, and flew off.

'Best to be careful,' said Pike. 'We're here now, anyway.'

There was no sign of any gate or opening or window, or of any habitation. Something squealed and ran off, and Simon hoped it was a rat and not anything worse.

'It's a dead end,' said Flora, feeling the sunsword girded underneath her robe, and suddenly suspicious of Pike.

'To you, maybe,' answered Pike. He kneeled by the wall, and counted the bricks along from the right, and pushed one in. There was a clicking sound, and something shifted, and stuck, and then shifted again.

A small gap opened slowly in the wall. 'There you go,' said Pike. 'Nothing special. Just a secret door.

Come on, go in. You two first.' He glanced around again, but could see nobody watching from above or from the entrance to the alley. Simon ducked inside, then Flora slipped through, and Pike scrambled in last. He checked behind him again one last time.

They were in a small, cold corridor, lit by a silver torch. When Pike closed the door, they were plunged into near-darkness, and Simon became afraid.

'Walk straight on,' came Pike's voice.

Not that there's anywhere else to go, thought Simon. He groped his way along for a while, each moment in time stretching further and further. *I feel like I'm always in darkness*, he thought. *Always in shadow.* He remembered Anna in that long red dress, her frightened face.

He stepped forwards, reaching for Flora's hand behind him. And just as he found her comforting touch, he ran into something.

Or someone.

'Intruders,' said a voice. A flickering light appeared, then another. At Simon's eye level was a large expanse of cloth and armour, which he assumed could only be worn by a person. A very tall, very strong person, who was holding a weapon and pressing it into him. The point of a knife was digging into his stomach. He gasped in shock.

Two others emerged from the darkness. 'You're coming with us,' said the first man. Simon felt strong arms heft him up, heard Pike's cry of protest, and then he was being carried in a fireman's lift.

Simon couldn't see very much, being upside down as he was. A few minutes later, he was dumped on to a freezing, wet stone floor, and Pike and Flora were thrown down next to him. They were obviously in a cave underground.

'You don't understand,' said Pike, as the three men levelled their weapons at them. 'I'm –'

'We'll see who you are in a moment,' said one of the men gruffly, before heading off into the darkness.

They waited, listening to drips of water splashing around them, hearing echoes of voices and footsteps. The two remaining guards did not seem that bothered by them, but were alert, their hands ready at their sword belts.

Simon heard footsteps approaching, and a new, strangely muffled voice spoke. 'Well,' it said. 'You took your time. But you've brought them to me, just as we planned.'

What the hell? thought Simon, hairs prickling all over his body.

Pike stiffened and sat up. The weapons moved away. More lamps appeared along one side of the cave, casting a long shadow on the ground. It was that of a man, and the man's head bore horns.

The Broken King, thought Simon. *He's here. He's got us already.* Simon flicked Flora's hand, ready to try to get up and run, and felt Flora stiffen in anticipation.

The shadow melted into the greater darkness as the figure came forwards. It loomed in front of them, lit by the silver lamps – a tall, horned figure with a sword.

Pike was standing up, walking, now running, towards the figure. He reached it, paused.

And then he embraced it.

Much to Simon and Flora's surprise, the figure returned the embrace.

'Get up, get up, both of you,' said Pike, his voice full of joy. 'This,' he said, taking off from the figure what was now, obviously, a horned helmet, 'is my father's sister. Lady Lavinia, the Lady of the Stag.'

It was a woman, her face gaunt and lined, her hair fine silver. A stag at bay was embossed on her frontlet, and she moved fluidly and quickly, like a deer, her eyes large and dark and liquid and wild. There was something tight and controlled, though, in her body.

She did not look like she wasted any energy.

'These are they?' she said to Pike.

Pike nodded. 'Yes, my lady. They're the ones.'

'These two?' she said, sounding surprised. 'Are you sure you got the right ones? I must say, I was expecting them to be . . . bigger. Stronger, certainly. How old are they? Have they fought before?'

Why is she so surprised? thought Simon. He stood up and straightened himself, and Flora did the same.

'So,' said Lavinia. 'You two . . . children are the ones who are going to do it.'

'Do . . . what?' said Flora. 'Nice to meet you by the way. I'm Flora, and this is –'

'I know who you are,' Lavinia interrupted. 'You mean my nephew here hasn't told you?'

'I haven't had much time to get things straight,' said Pike apologetically.

'Huh,' snorted Lavinia. 'Then I'd better explain quickly. You, my children, are special. You are the ones we have been waiting for. You are the ones who are going to free us from tyranny. The two from the other land, the place in-between, who will come to seek their siblings, and with the sunsword and the hunting horn tear the king's shadow and overthrow the Broken King.'

Simon gasped and caught Flora's expression of wonder. 'We . . . We didn't . . .'

'What do you mean, the king's shadow?' said Flora sharply.

'It is his protection,' answered Lavinia. 'He made it with deep, secret words that he learned from the mysteries in the centre of the worlds . . . They say that he took it from the robe of the Threefold Goddess herself . . . Nothing can tear through it but the sunsword and the hunting horn. And there is a further problem. Those weapons, to work on the king, must be wielded by people from your world.'

The Threefold Goddess, wondered Simon. *The mysteries at the centre of the worlds* . . . It was dizzying, all this new knowledge, and these strange and wonderful hints of things that ran deeper than he might ever have known.

'No time to lose,' said Lavinia brusquely. 'The king gets worse by the day. We'd better get you to the princess as quickly as possible. Have you sent the signal?'

Pike shook his head.

'Then do it. Do it now.' And she pulled a knife from her belt, and stalked purposefully towards Pike.

Chapter Seven

THE
BLESSED ONES

'YOU SHOULDN'T HAVE have done it.' Anna was hunched in the corner of the echoing room where she and Johnny were kept prisoner, bounded by three black, shimmering walls that only opened to let in the king or his attendants – Bruin the giant, Malek the dwarf, sometimes Andaria the rider, who wore a long green cloak and stared at them distantly, as if she couldn't quite see them, and scowled at them when she did.

Sometimes the chattering monkey creatures would come in with the other attendants, and scamper round, tease them and pull their hair. Nobody had named them, and nobody seemed to know where they were from. It was these creatures that Anna hated the most, because she couldn't understand them, or what they wanted.

The fourth wall was made up of windows, out of which they could see on to the square below. It was currently empty.

Their prison had no furniture apart from a low, black daybed. Anna had been sleeping on it; Johnny had made a corner his own, as far as he'd been able.

Johnny was standing at the window, his hands clenched. He looked ravaged and tired. He was scratching his arms.

'I would have come back for you, if I'd escaped. I'd have found help.'

'No, you wouldn't.' Anna slumped down. 'You're just like Simon.'

'You don't know that,' said Johnny savagely. He turned. He had bags under his eyes and was shivering, his eyelids twitching. He muttered something under his breath.

'What if you died?' said Anna. 'It's pointless. That's what Bruin says.'

'And what else does Bruin say?' said Johnny.

'More than you know,' said Anna. She played with

her coronet for a while, trying it on and looking at herself in the glass. Her reflection hung, suspended, above the buildings below, and it suddenly made her frightened.

'Bruin said that one girl did escape.'

'And who was that?' Johnny steepled his fingers across his chest – a habit which particularly annoyed Flora, and which annoyed Anna now.

'I'm not telling you,' said Anna. 'You're stupid.'

'Anna, come on. Tell me. There might be some information in the story. Something we can use!' The light returned to Johnny's eyes, and the eagerness in his expression made Anna relent.

Looking away from him, she said, 'Well . . . I can't remember exactly, but . . . he said a girl did escape.'

'Who? How?' said Johnny, moving towards Anna. 'Please! Try to remember!'

'I can't!' said Anna.

'What was her name?'

Anna sniffed. 'She was called . . . Harriet. And . . . And she was torn apart by the royal hounds and she died and nobody ever saw her again. So there! We're stuck here in this stupid prison in . . . the stupid land of the stupid Broken King and I want to go home!' She was on the verge of crying, but she decided against it.

'Yeah, yeah,' said Johnny dismissively, feeling instinctively that he shouldn't encourage her. 'We're in a children's book. But *where* are we? Are we in a different dimension? A different planet? How do we get home? We were brought here . . .'

Taken here, thought Anna. *No, sent here . . . Simon sent me here.* Something unpleasant uncoiled inside her and overwhelmed all other thoughts. *My own brother. He sent me here.* She felt a moment of pure rage. She remembered. The last rhyme Simon had said that night.

He'll come in blinding light.
He'll wrap you in the night.
Before the start of day
The Broken King will take you away!

The hand on her shoulder. The face, pure and pale. The sword, shimmering and sharp. A red tongue, poking through white teeth.

And then . . . not so much falling, but rushing. A great rush of things – stars, the moon, blackness, dizzying, other.

'Are we on the moon?' she said timidly.

Johnny snorted. 'Hah. Yeah, and Buzz bloody Aldrin's going to come and rescue us. Why don't we write *HELP* on a flag and wave it when we go outside? Or mark it out with stones or something? That's what they do in books, isn't it? Then NASA can spot it with their telescopes and send a shuttle and we'll all be home in time for tea.'

As Anna began to weep quietly, Johnny relented.

'I'm sorry,' he said, padding towards her and reaching out his arms.

Anna pushed him away. 'You, silly boy, tried to escape! In the middle of the day! He might kill us. Boys are so silly . . .'

'He hasn't killed us yet,' said Johnny, feeling repentant, and reminded forcefully of Flora when she was little. He was about to say more when the shadowy black wall shimmered and an opening appeared in it.

The pair of prisoners automatically stiffened and drew together. Johnny put his arms over Anna's shoulders, and she gripped his hands.

Out of the gap came Bruin, the giant. His long, light hair framed a furrowed and bearded face. He wore a black tunic and black boots. He was always armed, but Anna had never seen him even touch the hilt of his sword. He rarely spoke. He looked almost tenderly at the pair of them, and then turned and opened the gap in the shadowy wall wider.

'His Most Excellent and Immortal High Majesty, King Selenus of the Silver Kingdom, Keeper of the Kingdom of the Moon, Destroyer of the Golden Realm, Sunderer of the Realms, Friend of the Goddess and Protector of the People,' announced Bruin, his voice deep and slow.

Dressed in a swirling black robe embroidered with silver stars, his silver horns poking out on either side of his head, the king entered the room. The protective shadow that always clung around him was faintly present. He stroked it, absently.

His long, silver hair was wild, trailing behind him, floating as he walked, and his eyes glimmered with a crimson glow. He smiled, and his teeth shone wetly. A trail of black-clad servants followed him, who spread out and stood with their backs to the walls and their faces glazed over, staring straight ahead.

The king's horns always made Anna shiver; now she watched him, holding her breath, as he stalked round the room, peering into corners, and then out of the windows. She remembered a picture of a devil she'd seen in a book of fairy stories, and let out a sob of fear. Nobody paid any attention to her, apart from Johnny, who squeezed her shoulder.

'Scrapes in the sky,' said the king, enunciating the 's' sounds emphatically. 'Darkness. Meddling . . . meddling, scratching, I can feel it. Deep in the core, shadows twisting. Sometimes I feel her, in the shadow . . . Three things . . . Shattering, distorting, mutating . . .' The king's eyes rolled into the back of his head, and he put his hands on his cheeks. His knees trembled. He moved a little like a spider.

'What is he doing?' whispered Anna to Johnny.

Johnny shrugged.

'I see her . . . I see her lying there, and she is mine . . . Oh the things that I have done!' The king's voice came as if from far away, distant and strange. 'The secrets I have learned . . .' He spasmed, violently, and almost fell. Bruin went to stop him, and the king, as suddenly as he had gone into his trance, snapped out of it. 'What are you looking at?' he spat, turning on Bruin.

Bruin simply bowed his head, released the king, and waited for him to move his attention elsewhere. The stars on his robe caught the king's eye, and he twirled round, sparkling, laughing.

Anna looked away. Johnny stood mute, arms folded. He was thin and exhausted.

'The stars are purest silver thread,' called the king,

'beaten to the finest possible thinness. A spider's web, they tell me, is no finer. Spiders . . .' He went to the window again and looked out. 'Legs, scuttling . . . Webs, catching . . . Flies, ready to be consumed . . . I have put down webs . . . What are they doing out there, in the far places? Do they shiver at my name? My shadow has reached the ends of my kingdom, and it presses upon the Realm . . .'

Anna's face darkened when she saw what was coming through the door after the king. It was the dwarf, Malek, pushing what Anna thought of only as the Contraption. When Malek passed Anna, Anna turned away. Malek was dressed identically to Bruin. What the king had once found so amusing about them was that they looked alike, with Malek being a female, miniature version of Bruin.

The king spun round. 'Silver. Such a charming metal,' he said gently, pacing to the centre of the room. 'Mine, of course. The Silver Kingdom. Note that down, somebody.' He looked around. Bruin cast about for something to write with. 'Note that down!' he said, louder. 'I said write it! Sayings of King Selenus. Oh why won't you do it? Silver is a charming metal.' With a swift sharp movement he pulled a thin blade concealed in his left horn and held it just in front of Bruin's eye.

Bruin gulped, blinked, and showed the king a notebook.

'At last. Have it printed,' sniffed the king, 'and placed in every home.' He shoved the blade back into his horn, and clapped his hands together. Bruin signalled to a servant who scurried away.

Malek the dwarf was busying herself with the Contraption. It was a simple metal box with two tubes extending out of it. One was going to be placed on the skin of the Blessed Ones. The other would be attached to the king.

Anna hated those tubes.

'Now, my darlings,' said the king, and smiled expansively. He looked at Johnny. Handsome, gaunt, worn-out Johnny. Johnny turned away, running a hand through his black, scruffy hair.

'I think it's your turn,' said the king, and moved over to where Johnny was standing and forcibly turned him so that they were face to face. He drew his finger down Johnny's cheek, first along the normal side, and then along the silvery substance that had replaced his skin. It was all Johnny could do not to flinch.

'I'm still wondering where this came from . . .' whispered the king quietly. 'And who would take your skin? You say you can't remember . . .'

Johnny shook his head. 'I can't. I woke up, and . . . I didn't even notice until I looked in the mirror.' This was true.

The king sniffed the air, then released Johnny. 'Well, Johnny, you'd better get ready.'

In spite of herself, Anna relaxed. She was terrified of the machine, and what it did to them. It seemed to suck the very life out of their bones.

'Come on, now,' said the king softly. He took Johnny by the hand. Johnny sagged, and hung back a little. 'What's the matter now, Johnny?' said the king. 'Such a funny name. Johnny!'

'I . . .' Johnny stopped, not wanting to antagonise the king. The truth was, he wasn't sure he could take it. He'd been withdrawing since they'd arrived here, and that . . . Contraption, as Anna called it, wasn't helping. He was weak – weaker than he'd ever been, his limbs aching all the time, and his dreams . . . His dreams were worse than what he saw around him when he woke up.

But he couldn't let the king do it to Anna. That would not be fair. She was too little. He, on the other hand, could take it. He stiffened himself.

'I'm ready,' he said.

The king nodded, and led him to the Contraption, and connected the tubes. Johnny braced himself.

'Turn it on,' said the king.

Malek flicked a switch, and Anna shut her eyes and began to shudder in sympathy with Johnny.

We have to escape, she thought. *That girl Harriet at least got out of the palace. We have to find out what she did. And we have to do what she did. And not get eaten by the royal hounds . . . It's the only way. Or . . .*
She blinked her eyes open and saw Johnny, shaking, and the king, arms outstretched, drinking in the life force that he took from them.

Or soon, we'll be killed.

Chapter Eight

THE

TEMPLE CAVE

L AVINIA, THE LADY of the Stag had almost
reached Pike, her knife outstretched, when there
was a small commotion. In came a girl, a little older
than Flora, skinny and alert-looking, in an absurdly
fine embroidered dress and holding a heavy mace.
'My name's Eagret,' she said, looking coldly at Simon
and Flora. 'And look who I found skulking about.'
She pulled someone by the wrist into the light. It
was another girl, taller and quiet, wearing a long,
crimson dress and who had clearly been crying. 'It's
Scarlet, the daughter of the Crimson Knight.'

Scarlet dropped to her knees. She was terrified.

'Please don't hurt me,' she said, so softly that Simon could barely hear her. There was a rustling and coughing from the others looming about the room. Lavinia looked impatient.

'How did you find us? We haven't got time for this.'

'I know her,' said Pike, 'or used to, at least.' He made as if to go to the girl, but Lavinia prevented him.

'You don't know her now,' said Lavinia sharply. 'Speak, girl.'

'I . . . I didn't know . . . I had heard of something like you, and I just ran and ran when they took him away . . . I didn't want to see it happen. He never hurt anyone . . .'

'I was watching for her, my lady. I knew her before,' said Eagret, tenderly stroking Scarlet's hair.

'You can vouch for her?'

'I can,' said Eagret.

'Swear her in, quickly. She doesn't look up to much,' harrumphed Lavinia. Pike ran to Scarlet, and she grabbed him, sobbing.

Simon was hungry and thirsty. He swigged from one of the two plastic bottles of water they still had, and passed it on to Flora. Pike's aunt looked strangely at the bottle, then pressed her lips together.

'Enough of this weeping.'

Scarlet wiped her eyes, and Pike released her.

'Do you swear on the Threefold Goddess that you will tell nobody of us, that you will disclose this place to no one, that you will work with us to overthrow the king and restore the Kingdom to its former glory?' said Lavinia.

Scarlet sniffed, screwed up her face, and said, hardly faltering, 'I swear.'

Eagret raised her up and there was a murmur of approval from the crowd. She looked bedraggled and hopeless in her long red dress. 'Let's get you some weaponry,' said Eagret, and led her off. Scarlet's dress swept the floor as she left, and one of the boys watching pretended to trip over it, laughing and making a face.

'There aren't many of us,' Pike's aunt was saying. 'What you see is everyone in our cause.' Simon and Flora looked around the cave, now lit by a few more torches. There was a scattering of people, maybe ten or eleven in total: the three tall young men who had met them in the passage, and girls and boys of varying ages. Some were dressed in fine clothing that shone with silver and gold threads, and were embroidered with the shapes of animals; others were in all but rags. They held an assortment of weapons – a few daggers, spears, an axe or two and a scattering of bows and arrows. Others had ploughshares and rakes and hammers. They all shared one thing: a haunted expression in their eyes, and deep circles under them.

'We are mostly relatives of those Taken Apart by the king,' she said. 'Or those wronged by him. We live here, in the temple cave, where it's safe. It's an ancient, holy place, dedicated to the Threefold Goddess. There were priests here once, before the king executed them all, but there remains some protection from when it was a temple. The royal hounds cannot reach us, nor the king's magehawks. Nobody comes here, except us,' said Lavinia, quelling the group. 'Now send the signal,' she said, brandishing the knife again at Pike.

Pike looked grim. 'Everything that comes in and out of the palace is searched or sensed,' he said. 'They can detect anything artificially made – metal, paper, so on.'

'So how will you get your message into the palace?' asked Flora.

Pike went white – whiter than he usually was.

Flora realised. 'The skin-map . . .'

'The map could only be copied on to skin to get it

out of the palace. Now . . . I wouldn't watch this, if I were you. Look away.' Pike gestured at them.

Simon and Flora did as they were told, and turned towards one of the cave's walls. There was a recess, like in the temple of Mithras, and a low flat stone – what must have been an altar. It was bare of ornament, and there was no statue on it.

What god was worshipped here long ago? thought Simon, and he shivered. *The threefold goddess . . . What was she? Where is she now?* He heard the sound of something metal being brought out, maybe from a sheath. He caught Flora's eye and winced. Then there was a shout from Pike, which he suppressed quickly.

'You can look now,' said Lavinia, a few minutes later. Pike's arm was bandaged up, and he was wincing. He smiled ruefully at Simon and Flora.

'It'll heal in no time,' he said.

Lavinia was stretching out something, which Simon assumed was Pike's skin, bending over it with great attention. Pike came over to Flora and Simon, and Simon put a hand on Pike's shoulder and gripped it gently. His head was beginning to swirl a little. Pike looked so different now – his cheekbones were sharp, his hair glossy and curly.

Simon glanced at Flora. *Do we look different here?* he thought. Flora was a little more wiry than usual, it was true. He inspected his own hand. A bit skinnier, perhaps, but maybe that was because he hadn't eaten properly for a while.

Lavinia turned round and presented Pike with a small packet.

'The signal,' she said gravely.

Pike whistled. Out of the darkness came a bird. The shadows shifted around it, and Simon recognised it as one of the sort he'd seen earlier when hiding by the square. A white-eyed magehawk.

Pike gave the packet to the bird's beak, and whispered something to it. It seemed to shift, and then dissolve.

'Specially trained,' said Pike. 'He'll appear just outside the palace and fly over the appointed place. If Selena responds within an hour, we'll know that we can meet her later. If not . . .'

'Then what?' asked Flora.

'Then there's trouble,' said Pike.

'We must prepare for the worst,' said Lavinia. 'There are spies everywhere. Nothing is safe.'

Those bleak words echoing behind her, she strode off into the caves.

Chapter Nine

THE ROOM
OF WONDERS

SELENA, THE SILVER Princess, was sitting in her private library in the tower by her sleeping chamber when she sensed movement at her window. A flash, as quick as thought. She looked around. Clara, her attendant, was lazily leafing through some coloured prints of grand dances that had taken place in the palace in the years before the king's troubles, and hadn't noticed. Casually, Selena got up and paced over to the shelves by the window.

'It's such a shame,' she said, knowing that Clara wouldn't care, 'that the works of the Icebound poets were mostly destroyed in the fire in the temple of

Boreas, isn't it? We have so few of them left.'

Clara murmured something without looking up, and Selena took the opportunity to pick up the little packet that had been left on the sill. She slipped it into the embroidered bag she kept on a string round her waist. She'd have to look at it later. Her whole body was alive with energy and anticipation. She knew what was in there. She saw the magehawk outside the window, which briefly acknowledged her with its white eyes, then vanished. Her heart thrummed.

She didn't even know if she could trust Clara – good, simple Clara, who'd been her attendant since they were little girls play-fighting with baby swords in the palace rooms.

Without twitching a muscle in her face, she said, 'Oh, Clara, could you go and find out when my fencing tutor is coming? I've forgotten if it's today or tomorrow.'

Clara, keen to get out of the library, closed the book of prints, stood up, bowed, and left.

As soon as she'd gone, Selena took out the packet and unrolled it, her fingers trembling. There it was, written in blood, on some skin that had been cured like leather by that horrible process she'd done herself for the skin-map. It was the symbol they'd agreed on. A pair of horns with an arrow through them.

They're in the temple cave, she thought. *By the Threefold Goddess, I must act immediately.*

She heard a cough behind her and almost jumped. Instead she put the message back into her pouch, picked up a copy of one of the Icebound poets' work, and turned round as if brought out of some deep thought.

It was Sir Mark, the Knight of the Swan. She gasped inwardly. How long had he been there?

He smiled and bowed. He was wearing a black tunic, and it was figured with silver swans. 'I see you have a fondness for poetry,' he said. 'I like the Indigo poets, myself.'

Careful, thought Selena. *What does he mean? Don't say anything that can be interpreted in any other way.*

'It passes the time,' she said. 'When I am not involved in serving the king, my father, of course.'

'Everything we do serves the king,' said the Knight of the Swan.

'Now, what brings you here?' said Selena, trying not to appear wrong-footed as the knight turned over the covers of a couple of books. She walked as smoothly as she was able towards a plush, comfortable sofa, and sat down. Here she felt more at ease.

'I saw Clara on an errand in the corridors, so thought I would tell you myself.'

What fresh horror have you brought? thought Selena.

'His Majesty wants to see you,' said the knight.

'You have come back from the other world,' said Selena.

'I have,' replied the knight. 'The intruders, Simon and Flora, crossed into the Kingdom, but were not seen at point of entry. The gap closed behind them, and I returned through my swans. The renegades' helper, Giles Cuthbertson, remains behind. The other . . .' The knight struggled for a second.

'There was another?'

'I'm . . . not sure,' said the knight. He sounded disappointed with himself.

Good, thought Selena. *It worked. The knight didn't recognise Pike, and maybe didn't even see him.*

'Why were they not seen?' said Selena, trying to appear stern.

Sir Mark's face remained impassive. 'Because the soldiers were engaged upon a glorious exercise, attacking the woods and the earth.'

He's so loyal, thought Selena. *I can't trust him more than I would trust a poisonous snake.* 'Well then,' she said. 'We must fulfil our duty. Take me to him.'

'He is in the Room of Wonders.'

Selena got up and strode out of the library. She'd

promised to reply to the message within the hour. She'd have to finish this audience as quickly as possible, and find somewhere she could be on her own. She marched through the corridors of the palace, over the thick, black rugs, past the tall windows that looked out on to the square below, past the heavy double doors of the king's chambers. She went through the main hall, and the throne room where her father announced his decrees to her. Every shadow, every movement, she observed and remembered. Sir Mark paced close behind her, and everyone scattered as they went.

She pushed through the huge glass doors that led into the Room of Wonders.

Her father was sitting on the tall silver chair in the middle of the chamber. At his feet were the two Blessed Ones: the older boy, Johnny, and the small girl, Anna. Johnny was a man, really, thought Selena, studying him. He was certainly handsome, but in a different way from the men who proclaimed themselves her suitors. Not that anyone had dared to do so recently . . . And Anna had a sweetness about her, an innocence that tugged at Selena's heart. *But she has lost that innocence now,* thought Selena, *after all she has seen.*

The little monkey creatures were skittering by the window, playing with a curtain, draping it around themselves and howling with amusement. Bruin the giant was on one side of the room, Malek the dwarf on the other. Both bowed as she entered – Bruin smiling sadly, Malek merely blinking. She acknowledged them, and inclined her head to her father, who waved a hand airily, his protective shadow slipping around his skin.

The only thing that could tear that shadow was the sunsword, Selena reminded herself, and the only thing that could keep it torn open was the hunting horn. Nobody from the Kingdom or the Golden Realm could do it. It was only these people from the place in-between . . . That was why Simon and Flora were so important.

Selena was shocked to see that the Blessed Ones were attached to the throne by thin silver chains. *That's a new development*, she thought, and kept her face immobile. The little girl, Anna, shivered, and her chain jingled.

She glanced around. The room, apart from the throne, was entirely empty. *The Room of Wonders*, she thought. *Another of my father's follies*. There was nothing wondrous in it at all.

'Your Most Excellent High Majesty,' she said. 'I take great pleasure in coming to see you . . .'

'Yes, yes,' hissed the king, tapping his foot. His

eyes were gently glowing red, and he was fiddling with his left horn. His long face was white and elastic, his mouth opening to enunciate every syllable carefully, revealing his scarlet tongue. 'Mysteries in the shadows. A shattered statue, a peacock feather floating down, the world spinning into darkness . . . I see a crown on the stone . . .' His eyes glazed over and the room held its breath. There was no telling what he might do when his attention came back.

Then his face returned to normal, or what passed for normal. 'I have right cause to be wrathful,' he said, using his most courtly tones. He shook his head, his horns making elegant curves in the air.

Selena's whole body stiffened. Was this it? Was he going to declare war on the Golden Realm now?

'What do you mean, father? Have I displeased you?'

'No, no, not you,' said the king. 'It is aught to do with you, my daughter. These . . . people. These children, these little snivelling bratkins from the other world. The intruders. They asked for their siblings to be taken. And so I dispatched someone to take them. I control the way. None can come here from the Golden Realm or the place in-between without me allowing it. But Anna and Johnny are now mine. That's how it works, isn't it? They belong to me.' His voice was measured.

'Yes, father. That was how it started, so long ago, when the treaty was made.'

'And in my most gracious, most serene kindness, I declared that anyone who solved the three tasks of the shadow, the sun and the air could come and get their sibling back, did I not?'

'You did, your majesty,' said Selena.

'As I should, in my most merciful clemency. But,' said the king, 'there is some difficulty. These ones here are . . . useful. They provide me with power.' He jerked on the chains, causing Anna and Johnny to totter a little. 'And their siblings had help from the Realm.' He stood up. Selena inwardly tensed. The expression on her father's face changed into the one she had grown to fear. 'Which *isn't allowed.*' He was so motionless it was even more frightening, his face a mask, his eyes shining redly. 'It's *not fair* if people don't abide by the rules.' He took two blades from his horns and held them at arm's length, looking ready to hurl them at anyone who said the wrong thing. Selena felt she might choke on her tongue.

Then, languidly, the king sat down once more, replaced the blades in his horns, and sniffed, folding his hands together into his lap. 'I sent you, my dearest daughter, because I thought you would not fail me.

You fought them – where the sunsword was hidden, along with that . . . *thing* from the Golden Realm – Mithras?'

Selena nodded, and swallowed.

'Then tell me . . .' The king stood up again, drew out one of the shiny blades from his horns, and paced slowly towards Selena, playing with it all the time. It was as thin as a wire and would cut Selena's throat with ease. He came to a stop just within reach of her. She felt a bead of sweat trickle down her neck and almost moved. 'Why did they win?' He sounded uninterested, but Selena knew that was just for show.

She was prepared for this. 'They were too strong, your majesty. There were two of them. And somehow Mithras had escaped his bonds. When he came, I was overwhelmed.'

'That is not good enough,' said the king, 'for my own daughter. You know what the sunsword can do.'

The point of the blade came to within a finger's breadth of Selena's head. 'You know,' he said conversationally, 'that I could kill you with just a tiny bit of pressure here? This blade would push into your brain, and that would be the end of you.' He grinned. 'But forgive me, I digress.' He snatched back the blade and returned it to its horn. 'You and the Knight of the Swan – where is he?'

The knight stepped forwards from where he was waiting respectfully and bowed his head.

'You, my own daughter, and my most trusted Sir Mark, the Knight of the Swan, have both allowed these intruders into our kingdom. It is now upon your honour,' he said, 'to find them, and bring them to me. And I will make an example of them, and the Realm will know not to trouble us again!'

Anna, who'd been quietly listening carefully to everything, clamped a hand to her mouth and stifled back the sobs that had arisen. Was it Simon? Had he come to get her? How could she find out? The king had said intruders, hadn't he? How many were there? More than one? A tiny glimmer of hope began to shine within her.

Selena was trembling inside. This wasn't what she'd expected at all. She'd wanted her father to declare war immediately, and then she was going to use Simon and Flora to topple him, and form an alliance with the Realm.

Simon and Flora had the sunsword and the hunting horn. They could get through the king's shadow barrier as they were not of the kingdom. They would kill the king, and then she, with the might of the Golden Realm behind her, would become queen.

That was how it was going to work.

And Flora and Simon . . . What would happen to them? She knew, and she pushed the thought away.

'You and the Knight of the Swan shall investigate together and report back to me,' said the king.

Oh no, thought Selena. *How will I get the message to Pike now?*

The knight turned to Selena and bowed, his smooth face gleaming, his long black hair framing his face. 'Shall we begin, my princess?'

The knight took her arm, and, bowing to the king, led her away.

'We shall report back soon, your majesty,' said the knight, and they left the Room of Wonders.

Selena glanced behind her, but the doors were closed in her face. Time was short. The message burned in her pocket.

'Shall we start,' said the knight, 'with the informers in the city?'

Selena nodded grimly. She had to get out of this. 'Meet me at the side gate in ten minutes' time,' she said. 'In disguise.' And she swept away, leaving the knight appraising her with a quizzical expression.

Once in her chamber, she went to a secret drawer

in her desk where she kept a supply of cured skin, pricked her finger, quickly wrote her reply, and whistled the tune for the magehawk, which appeared outside her window. She pressed her message into its beak. As soon as it vanished, she collapsed into a chair, breathing deeply, and allowed herself a second or two of blankness before pulling herself up again and putting on some brown, shapeless clothes.

My father, she thought. *My father.* She remembered suddenly how he'd held her when she was little, and shown her how to ride on a horned colt that was gentle but strong. He'd been sane once, she'd heard. Beloved and glorious. There had been meetings with the Golden Realm, tournaments and dances. Until that day, long before she was born, when he'd started to go mad, and the first of the Takings Apart happened . . . Broken, they called him in the Golden Realm. The Broken King. He knew it too, but he did not care; he sometimes even revelled in the name.

Feeling the horror of it deeply in her heart, she strode out to meet the knight. She found him, waiting patiently, dressed in a simple grey robe. Without acknowledging him, she pushed through the doors and set off into the bowels of the city, the knight pacing mechanically behind her.

Maybe my father can be sane again, she thought. *Maybe I won't have to overthrow him after all. Maybe he can be persuaded to abdicate.*

But as she walked, she knew it couldn't be true. She counted the things that she did know, under her breath.

One. She knew that the king her father could not be mended.

Two. She knew that Flora and Simon would tear the king's shadow.

Three. She knew that when they broke the shadow, they would kill the king.

Four. She knew that when the king died, he would take his assassins with him. And they would die too.

It was inevitable as the silver sun rising the next morning, as the winds changing, as the swell of the sea breaking on the shore.

She was the only one who knew this last thing. Pike didn't know it, the Lady of the Stag didn't know it, nor any of the other rebels.

And it broke her heart to think it.

Oh, Father, she thought. *Oh my father, what have you done?*

Chapter Ten

THE

STEWARD'S HOUSE

'THAT'S IT, THERE,' Pike whispered, halting Simon in his tracks and making Flora bump into him.

'Sorry,' she said into his ear. 'Clumsy.'

They had been pacing through the narrow cobbled streets for some time now, keeping to the edges, and avoiding anything that moved or looked like it might move, for there were many things in the shadows, and their intent was not always to the good.

It was dark – Simon guessed about the middle of the night, if night was the same length here as it was back home – and colder than Simon had expected it to be. Their thin, coarse garments did little to keep out the biting breeze. There was a different light in the sky now, less bright than the one that shone during the day, but still silvery, with an edge of red that made everything seem slightly sinister. *But it's normal for them*, Simon reminded himself.

There were stars, too, but not in any constellation that Simon recognised. Sometimes a shape would flit over the moon, too big for a bat. Sometimes things would growl and skitter away into the dark. They'd left the sunsword and the hunting horn in the temple cave, and Simon felt exposed with nothing but a dagger for protection.

Pike was pointing to a low building in front of them that looked boarded up and dilapidated. He told Flora and Simon to wait where they were, under the eaves of a house, then he went cautiously up to the door. He tried it, found it locked, pulled out a key, opened it and disappeared briefly before reappearing and signalling to them to come over.

Scanning the road and seeing nothing stirring, Simon and Flora pattered across the street to join Pike. As soon as they'd come in, Pike shut and locked the door. 'Through here,' whispered Pike.

'Where are we?'

'This is a house that used to belong to my father,' said Pike. 'Our steward lived in it. Now it's deserted. We chose it as a place to meet because there's a ban on anyone coming here.'

'Why's that?' said Simon.

'One of the king's decrees. Anything to do with a dishonoured knight is made out of bounds. His property is confiscated by the king, his children . . .' Pike paused. 'I heard something . . . something moving . . .'

A voice came out of the darkness. 'Nobody would think that the son of a shamed knight would come back to his father's properties . . . Isn't there a charge on anyone who does so?'

Pike, Flora and Simon formed a triangle, back to back, daggers drawn.

'Isn't it death?' continued the voice. It was low, soft, musical even.

'Who's that?' said Pike. 'Show yourself!'

A dim silver lamp appeared, and lit up a girl's face.

Pike sighed with relief. It was the princess. 'We got your message,' he said.

'We haven't got much time,' she said. 'I know that I am being watched.'

'Wait!' said Pike. 'Out of the darkness I come . . .'

'And into the light I go,' replied Selena.

'Password,' said Pike, answering Simon's enquiring expression. 'I'm sorry, your highness.'

'I know,' said Selena. 'Now we must get ready, quickly. The Blessed Ones are kept under close guard, and nobody is allowed in or out of their prison except the king himself and his attendants. At the Ceremony of Sundering –'

'You tried to kill us!' said Flora, interrupting suddenly. 'Why should we listen to anything you have to say?'

'It was necessary,' said Selena sharply. 'I had to fight you. If anyone else had done it, there is no doubt that you would be dead, Mithras would still be in his prison, and we would have no hope of . . .' She paused, considering. 'The Ceremony of Sundering is taking place soon. That is beyond the city, by the standing stone that marks the boundary. I hope to –'

'Hope is a fine thing,' said another voice – calm, distant, proud.

Everybody froze.

A light flared, flooding the room with a pale sheen. Simon saw Selena fully now, dressed in a long cloak with a hood, before he snapped round.

There, stepping casually across the room, was a man with dark hair, and a crooked, sensual smile across his handsome face. Simon gasped, and Flora tensed up.

Selena said calmly, 'Sir Mark. And, pray, what brings you into the city on a night like this?'

'Princess,' he said, stopping a few paces away from them. 'I lost track of you for a while. And then found you here . . . I waited to see what you were doing. I wonder what your father will say when he hears of this?'

'You don't know what you heard,' said Selena.

'I've always wanted to say, "We meet again",' said Sir Mark, ignoring her and moving closer to Simon and Flora. 'And you,' he continued, more menacingly, pointing at Pike. 'I couldn't see you properly before. You're the one that helped them, aren't you? Yes, you're Pike. The spawn of the traitor Knight of the Shark.'

'He was no traitor!' said Pike. 'He wouldn't kill an innocent woman, and he was Taken Apart because of it.'

'He disobeyed his king!' The knight's words cascaded over Pike's. 'That makes him a traitor. And there is nothing worse than that, in all the three worlds. You see,' he said, turning to Flora and Simon, 'you needed the approval of someone from the Kingdom to enter it – and since none of us would give it, our friend Pike here did.'

The Knight of the Swan paused, sniffed, and shook his black hair, almost daintily. 'Three children,' he sniffed. 'Hardly my idea of revolutionaries. But of course you two,' he pointed at Simon and Flora, 'didn't know what you were getting into, did you, when you said the rhyme . . . You know, your sister Anna cried for a day when they brought her in.'

'Is she all right?' asked Simon. 'Tell me! Have you hurt her? Has he hurt her?'

'She is blessed,' said the Knight of the Swan. 'You call for the king, and he sends a knight who takes the Blessed Ones, and they give the king power. But you're not meant to come and get them back. That doesn't happen. That has never happened, and it will not happen.'

'Well, you're wrong,' said Simon, surprising himself. 'We've come to get them. And we will.'

The knight laughed. 'Oh, Simon, I almost don't want to tell you, you look so . . . Well, in other circumstances, I would admire your courage. Now I think you're a little bit stupid. The Golden Realm has been using you, Simon. Or didn't you realise that?'

What? thought Simon.

'I can see from your expression that you haven't got the tiniest sliver of an idea about what's really going on here. Why do you think they helped you so much?'

'I . . . I don't know,' said Simon. 'I don't know what you're talking about. They didn't use us. We did it. I did it. I found the rhyme, I called the Broken King to take Anna. The Realm helped us, because . . .' He faltered.

Slowly and deliberately, the knight pulled his sword out of his scabbard, and looked down the length of it, ignoring Simon.

'So, your highness,' said the Knight. 'I did not realise there was a renegade at such a high level. My duty is to my king. What is it going to be?'

'You are mistaken, Sir Knight,' said Selena slowly. She stepped forwards, away from Pike, Flora and Simon.

What's she doing? wondered Simon.

Selena pulled out her own sword with a flourish and levelled it. She bowed formally to the knight.

'I was merely completing my task. My father the king asked us to find the intruders. And I have done so. It necessitated a small amount of dissembling, but then you would understand that, Sir Knight.' She inclined her head delicately.

Simon's heart thumped and he drew closer to Pike and Flora. *We've got no chance against the two of them*, he thought. *No chance at all.*

'If you will allow me, I will escort them quietly to the palace, where I will present them to my father, the king. And then the necessary preparations will be made.'

'Highness, I should not have doubted you,' said Sir Mark, resheathing his sword. '

'No!' shouted Flora suddenly, looking at Selena. 'It can't be true, it can't be . . .'

Simon wasn't so sure any more. Everything seemed to be in flux. He didn't know who was on his side and who wasn't. Were the Knight of the Swan and Selena really working together?

Sir Mark said, 'I had become suspicious of you, Princess. I have been watching your movements very carefully for a while. But you were working for your father all along, I see.' He bowed. 'The honour is yours, your highness. Now, perhaps –'

Suddenly Selena, moving faster than Simon had ever seen anyone move before, kicked Sir Mark's feet out from under him, and pinned him down with the tip of her sword. He had no armour; the shock on his face was evident.

'Mistaken again, Sir Knight,' said Selena. She turned to the three friends. 'Help me with him.'

'Traitor!' shouted the knight. 'You are a traitor to your kingdom! To your father!'

Selena knocked him on the head with a heavy blow. Sir Mark spasmed, and was quiet.

'I was not expecting this,' she said, ashen-faced.

She frisked him, and threw two daggers to the three, hilts first. Pike took them.

'Let's carry him out the back. We have to hope he didn't tell anyone he was coming here. Have you heard anything else outside?'

They shook their heads.

'We'll bring him to the temple cave,' said Selena.

Simon grabbed the knight's legs, and Pike hefted him from under his arms, whilst Selena supported the knight from underneath. Flora opened the door, and closed it once they were through.

It was dark still. Selena went ahead, and Simon and Pike followed, with the knight's arms over their shoulders, praying that he wouldn't wake up. Flora went behind, keeping a sharp look-out as they slipped through the gloomy streets. Once they were startled by a small hound that sniffed them and scuttled off; once a magehawk boomed low to their right. They avoided the main thoroughfares.

They stumbled along, as quietly as they could. When they came to the entrance of the temple cave, Selena signalled to them.

'I must go. I have been foolish, and that greatly. Wait in this place until you hear from me.'

And before they knew it, she had disappeared into the night.

When they reached the secret door, they bundled the unconscious knight inside, and Simon and Pike sat on him in the cave whilst Flora ran to get reinforcements. Soon, they'd tied him up to a chair in one of the caves, and the Lady of the Stag was throwing cold water over him. Two of the older rebels stood guard on either side of him.

He spluttered awake, and looked around himself, barely blinking.

'What do you know?' snapped Lavinia.

The Knight of the Swan checked his wrists, which were bound behind him, and his ankles, which were attached to both front legs of the chair. 'Good knots,' he said, 'whoever did them.' He grinned lazily, and shook his black hair away from his gleaming white forehead.

'Silly little bratlings,' he spat suddenly, and Simon shuddered.

Flora was standing warily to one side of him, and Pike and the Lady of the Stag were squaring up to the knight, face on.

The knight was slender, his pale skin as white as a swan's feathers, wiry muscles rippling. Sometimes, or perhaps it was the light, it even looked as if he had feathers bristling on the surface of his skin. There was a silver locket on a chain around his neck. Simon wondered what was inside it. A tiny engraving of a swan decorated it – no, not a swan. A cygnet.

'The king will take notice that his best knight is gone,' said the knight. 'You have not been very careful. Did you truly believe nobody to be watching for rebels?'

The Lady of the Stag clenched her teeth and snorted. 'How can you serve him?' she said. 'After what he did? After what he does? With how many people he's killed for no reason at all! And the children . . . the children he's taken, all these years . . .'

The knight's expression set into stone. 'I am a loyal servant of the king,' he said. 'I swore an oath when I put on this armour, like every knight in the Silver Kingdom. Like you did, Lavinia, my Lady of the Stag. But where is your oath now? You have dishonoured your knighthood!'

'My oath was broken when he killed my brother Leandrus!' said Lavinia vehemently. 'My oath was broken when I saw Leandrus Taken Apart and hung from the trees, his body denied even burial! You talk to me of oaths. The king broke every vow he'd ever taken!'

'He kept to the terms of his treaty. I swore to serve my king all my life, to the best of my ability.' His voice, though quiet, was passionate, and Simon found himself strangely admiring it.

'You really think that the king will search for you? You think he'll even notice? Ha!' The lady laughed hollowly. 'I bet that at this very moment he's playing with the ones he calls blessed – those poor children he uses . . .'

'Those poor children whose siblings wished them away!' spat the knight. 'You didn't want them, did you?' He looked directly at Simon and Flora, who shifted uncomfortably. 'So they were taken away, as you wished. Ha. And now your friends are simply using you.'

Simon said sharply, 'What do you mean by that?'

Pike said, 'Don't listen to him,' at the same time as Lavinia said, 'He's lying.'

'No, what does he mean?' said Simon.

A grin spread over the knight's handsome face.

'Those books with the incantation you spoke to wish away your siblings – where do you think they came from?'

'*In the Land of the Broken King*? We . . . we've always had it,' said Simon.

'But where did it come from? Can you remember buying it?'

Simon thought. He couldn't. Had he been given it for a birthday? He wasn't sure. It had just . . . always been there in the house.

'And the rhyme . . . Did you notice anything about the rhyme?'

'I . . .' Simon recalled the thought that had struck him the night he'd wished Anna gone. The book – the words – they'd seemed different from usual. 'I felt . . . I thought . . . The idea came out of nowhere, and when I picked up the book – I remember now – I felt like I hadn't seen those words before . . .'

Flora gasped and put both hands to her face.

'And I felt . . .' she started.

'Like someone was making me do it,' they both said at the same time.

There was a moment of pure clarity in which Simon saw the knight smirking, and Lavinia looking concerned, and Pike jumping from foot to foot.

'What is he saying?' said Flora.

'I said, don't listen to him!' said Pike. 'He's trying to cause trouble.'

'How can I cause trouble with the truth?' snarled the knight.

'You mean you *made* us do this?' said Simon, turning to Pike and Lavinia, as anger wormed its way through his body.

'It's not . . . quite like that,' said Lavinia.

'What did you do?' said Simon, attempting to control his voice.

'Don't embellish it now,' said the knight.

Lavinia smacked the knight round the face with a heavily armoured glove. It left a vivid red mark on his cheek, but he barely flinched.

'We'll tell you,' sighed Lavinia. 'But not here.'

'You'd better be quick,' said the knight. 'The king will look for me. He will find me. And then your rebellion will be as nothing!'

'You two watch him,' said Lavinia to the guards.

'If he tries anything – and I mean anything – you have my leave to knock him out.'

The knight's laughter echoed in the caves as Lavinia led Simon, Pike and Flora away from him, further into the chambers of the temple cave. As they left, Simon turned back and saw the knight, his wolfish smile broad, staring right at him, eyes gleaming. He gulped and followed the others.

Lavinia, carrying a torch, took them to a chamber a hundred paces away from where the knight was tied up, and when she'd put the torch into a bracket in the wall, began pacing up and down, her hands behind her back, her head bent low. Pike sat on a stony ledge cut into the rock. Simon rested against the damp wall, whilst Flora squatted, biting her nails. The light was dim, and the cavern echoed all around them, the background drip of water constant.

'This is bad,' said Lavinia, sounding exhausted. 'Very bad. The knight's absence will indeed be noticed, and then they will start looking for him, and then . . .' She gestured helplessly at her own neck and drew a line across it. 'But better, I think, for us to have him. I'm sure the princess will think of something.'

'What can we do?' asked Simon.

An eerie sound came to them: the Knight of the Swan singing a ballad from his childhood.

'Oh tear down the flowers
Topple the trees
Empty the bowers
My darling's left me.'

The tune sounded familiar to Simon, like a Russian folksong, lilting and sad.

Flora said, 'Can't we strike quickly? Go to the palace now?' She rubbed her eyes. Simon nodded in agreement. Pike looked alarmed.

'Not without the princess. How can the three of us break into the palace? She's the only one who can help. But I'm not sure how long it will be before the knight tries something . . .'

'What do you mean?' said Flora.

'He has certain powers that others of us don't have. That's partly why he's been so popular with the king. I'm not sure I know their full extent. I'm not sure anybody does.'

'I've seen him turn into a swan,' said Simon.

'Yes, shapeshifting is his main talent. It's a rare ability that occurs only once every generation or so. It takes a lot of energy, though, and he's tired now. I can't turn into a stag, although I wish I could . . .

Though there are many in the Golden Realm that have the capability.'

'Raven and the Flames,' said Flora.

'You mean the supporters of Mithras?' asked the Lady of the Stag. 'Yes, that is true. But the Knight of the Swan can do things with shadows that I cannot, that few can . . . He knows things, deeper things, about the worlds . . . He learns them from the king, who sees far into the inner parts . . . More than I could ever know.'

'But wait,' said Simon. The idea had been growing in his mind, getting too large and uncomfortable for him to hold it inside any longer. 'What the knight said – it's true, isn't it?' Deep anger was bubbling in his stomach. 'All this time, you were using us.' The people around him seemed to be getting larger, closing in on him, the walls of the cave to slide up and down. Everything was coming to a point, hard and cold. Pike seemed menacing, perching on the ledge, even Flora looked different to him.

Lavinia put her hands together carefully and smiled. 'We didn't . . . *use* you. You were the ones we noticed, and the ones who were most likely to call the Broken King, and so we . . . adapted our plans accordingly.'

'You gave us the words,' said Flora flatly, scrambling to her feet, an edge of fury in her tone. 'You put the words into our mouths. And you're using us now. We're here for his sister and my brother, but you've got other intentions. He – the knight – mentioned war. What does he mean?'

'I can't tell you any more. What we've decided must remain secret. Too much is known by too many already.'

Anger walled up inside Simon, blocking his thoughts like a heavy weight of concrete. He felt as if he was swimming against a strong tide. *I've got to get out of here*, he thought.

'Fine. In that case, I'm going to do this on my own,' Simon said furiously, the words spitting out of him. 'If you need me that much, you should at least bother to tell me everything.'

He blindly picked up his rucksack and ran out into the twisting caverns, the knight's song following him plaintively as he went.

He knew it was stupid, but he couldn't take it any longer. How could he be just a little cog in a machine whose purpose he didn't even know?

In the passageway outside he came to a place where the way branched. *Idiot*, he cursed himself, unsure of which way to go. He turned left and went down a path he thought might lead to the exit.

And then what? he thought. *Go out into the city, enter the palace, find Anna, and take her home? Like I can do that on my own . . .*

He came abruptly round a corner and stopped in his tracks.

There, sitting on a chair, bound and gagged, was Selena, the Silver Princess.

Chapter Eleven

THE WAY BETWEEN
THE WORLDS

PRINCESS SELENA JERKED her head, and Simon, discomfited, rushed forwards and ungagged her.

'What's happening?' asked Simon. 'I thought you'd gone back to the palace.'

Selena said, 'The other rebels came for me. They tricked me. They do not trust me. I am the daughter of the king, after all.'

Simon was entranced by her beauty and her voice – soft, silvery and gentle. The chamber they were in was small. Selena's feet were bound together with rope, and her hands tied behind her back. She shifted against her bonds.

'Are you all right?' said Simon feebly. 'Does it . . . hurt?' He stood immobile. What should he do? Should he release her? Maybe if he set her free she'd help him into the palace.

As if reading his mind, Selena said, 'Simon, you must release me. I can help you. We can go straight to the palace and find Anna.'

'But how do we get home after?'

'I know the answer to that,' said Selena. 'You have two shadow-spheres left, don't you? All you need to do is take the sunsword and the shadow-spheres and the horn back to where the standing stone is, do the same ritual backwards, and you'll be home.'

So I can *go home*, thought Simon. 'What about Anna?'

'She'll need the other shadow-sphere,' said Selena.

There was a little voice in Simon's head that wondered why the Lady of the Stag had tied up Selena without telling them.

'Things will all be better soon. When I am put on the throne in the king's place, and war is averted, then we will open the Way again.'

'What does that mean?'

'The Way is how we used to use to move between the three realms. We went freely, from one to another, and many passed along it. King Selenus closed off the Silver Kingdom when he sundered the realms. Those from the Golden Realm cannot reach here, and we cannot go there unless he wills it. But if we were to fully open the Way once more, and restore the worlds to their previous glory . . .' Selena paused and something dark flashed in her eyes. 'Help me now, Simon. Imagine, the Way open. You could travel to the Golden Realm, and see its beauties and its treasures . . . The Silver Kingdom would lie open once more and would live in freedom and pleasure. And as for your own world, you could bring people here, and you would learn and grow and become better . . .' Her voice became insistent, if anything a little harsh, and she flicked back her hair, fixing Simon with her eyes. 'Untie me, Simon, and we can escape, and you can take your darling sister back to the place in-between where you can live happily.'

For a moment Simon hesitated. There was something about her that he found disconcerting, but he couldn't quite put his finger on it. She smiled at him. That smile, that spellbinding smile.

The background echoes and splashes around him were making his head throb.

Yes, he thought. *I'll untie her, and we'll go straight*

to the palace and release Anna and Johnny and come back and get Flora . . . and then we'll open the Way.

He bent forwards and started fumbling with the ropes around her legs. *What thick boots she's wearing,* he thought. The ropes were tied very tightly and he couldn't get any purchase on the knot with his fingers.

'I might need a knife,' he said after a while. 'I'll go and get one –'

'No,' said Selena forcefully. 'Untie me now. We haven't much time.'

Simon tried again, and managed to prise loose a bit of the knot, which he tugged at.

'Yes, that's it,' said Selena.

The knot came undone, and Simon looked up, just as Selena kicked out at him fully on the chin, bending forward to undo the other leg. She'd worked her hands free already.

'Fool,' she said, standing up. The shadows in the room seemed to shiver a little. Selena advanced on Simon, hands outstretched, and then her hands were around his neck – strong hands, stronger than they ought to be, and his vision started to blur and it wasn't the princess looking down on him at all. It was the Knight of the Swan. Simon struggled and kicked but he couldn't breathe, he couldn't . . .

He's killing me, he thought, and everything started to go white.

Then there was shouting and confusion, and the pressure came off his neck. Simon fell and lay on his back, heard a struggle and voices – so dim and faraway they seemed – and then there was the familiar sight of Flora looking down at him, a worried expression in her eyes.

'Are you all right?' she said, helping him up.

Simon nodded. As he stood, Simon saw the knight being tied back in the chair, a lopsided grin on his face.

'Come on, Simon,' said Flora, tugging at him, but Simon couldn't help looking back as they left. 'You need to rest.'

And once more the Knight of the Swan began to sing.

The real Silver Princess had returned to her chamber in the palace immediately after she'd left Simon, Pike and Flora, fearing all the way back that guards would meet her there.

But when she reached her rooms, she found them empty. There was no light on in Clara's annexe.

Her pet hound stirred sleepily in the corner by her bed, and she reached out and stroked his head. He whimpered, snorted and settled back to sleep. There was no sign that anyone had noticed she had gone.

And that made her even more worried.

If they know, she thought, *and he's preparing some kind of trap for me . . . Tread carefully*, she thought.

She wept, and didn't sleep until the sun had almost risen.

Chapter Twelve

THE PLACE
IN-BETWEEN

'ON THE DAY of Sundering,' said the Lady of the Stag, 'there is a ceremony. The king takes the Blessed Ones to the standing stone, along with a few attendants, who will be armed. Of course, he is protected by his shadow; the arms are only for show. Nobody would dare to attack him that way.'

Simon sat listening, holding his knees, the hunting horn tucked under his arm. Flora was to his left with the sunsword laid flat on the ground in front of her, and Pike stood grimly with his back to them, facing out into the passageway. They could not risk their plans being overheard, not even by Eagret or Scarlet or any of the others who were slouching about the place.

'What's the ceremony for?' asked Simon.

'To celebrate the Sundering of the Realms,' said Lavinia. 'The day that the king forbade those of the Golden Realm to come to our kingdom, and the Way was blocked. He goes to the standing stone and blesses it. There, when he is in the middle of his praises, we can ambush him, release your siblings, and get you all home.'

Home, thought Simon. He felt a sudden movement in his pocket, and with surprise he pulled out Hover, the little bird-deer. Something was happening to it. Simon set it on the ground and they watched in fascination.

It was growing. Little by little, it was getting bigger and bigger. It shivered and shook its tiny head. And then its wings began to retract, its body to elongate, and it started to straighten up.

Before Simon could blink, standing in front of him was a person – a young man, entirely silver, androgynous, and clothed in a simple silver garment and with long silver hair.

Hover lifted his feet up and down, as if testing them, with some of the same delicacy that he'd had as a bird-deer. He shook all along his body, as if he were a dog just out of water, and then came towards Simon with a smile on his face. He bowed and extended his hands, then stood back up, his eyes strangely bright.

Simon reached out his hand, and Hover took it. Simon felt a jolt all along his arm, like when he'd first touched the bird-deer but much more muted.

'Well,' said the Lady of the Stag. 'That was unexpected. Where are you from?' she asked, addressing Hover.

Hover pointed to his mouth and shook his head, indicating that he couldn't speak.

'Where did you get him from?' asked Lavinia, looking at Simon with interest.

After the first task, when they'd eaten the shadow, and Simon was back sitting in front of his tent, he'd simply found Hover clasped in his hand. He told Lavinia so.

She still looked bemused. 'The hunting horn originates from here. The shadow-spheres are from the middle of the worlds. The sunsword was made in the Golden Realm, but it's the only thing from there that can function in the Kingdom. Anything else from the Golden Realm would have been immediately detected and taken to the king. There's something else here. Something I've never seen. Can you tell me exactly what happened?'

Simon thought back. 'Well, I did feel something small.'

'When? Describe exactly what happened.'

'I took it – him – out when we were in the cart, and I pressed him to my cheek . . .'

Lavinia marched up to Simon and took his face in her hands and examined his cheek. 'To this mark here?' She touched it. 'The messenger gave you this?'

Simon nodded, and was glad when Lavinia released him.

'I see. She imprinted you with some information. Hover picked it up when you touched him.'

'Like reading a computer program?' said Simon.

Lavinia looked blankly at him. 'Com-pu-ter?'

'Never mind,' said Simon. He was thinking that when the messenger had whipped him, it wasn't just a punishment.

'Is it like the Knight of the Swan?' asked Flora. 'I mean, is Hover?'

Lavinia shook her head. 'A shapeshifter? I don't know. But clearly he's been sent to help us. I hope,' she added distantly, a troubled look in her liquid eyes. 'He must have been waiting . . .'

Maybe, thought Simon, *he's a messenger too. That's*

what the people from the Golden Realm said they were. Messengers.

Flora said, 'I got whipped too. Do you think there's something in mine?'

'Perhaps,' said Lavinia. 'I imagine it will reveal itself in time.'

Hover settled himself down by Simon, who felt pleased at his nearness.

Lavinia continued with their plan. 'We will lie in wait among the rocks. Pike and I will attack the guards. Flora, you take the sunsword and slice through the king's shadow. Simon, you go with her and then blow the hunting horn. It will keep the shadow open. And then – you kill the king.'

There was silence in the room.

Then Flora spoke. 'So now what?'

'We wait for the ceremony,' replied Pike.

The Knight of the Swan had been removed to a further, darker part of the temple cave complex. He was now kept gagged, but when the gag was lifted so that he could be fed, he would always launch into the same song.

Though exhausted after his shifting, he still had energy to sing. His haunting, plaintive, melancholy voice echoed through the caverns and passageways and burrowed into Simon's mind, tainting his thoughts. *As it's meant to do*, he thought. Every time he heard it, he saw the knight in his memory, reaching out to him, arms outstretched, about to grab him by the throat.

Simon went to find a space by himself, away from the lounging, hard-eyed rebels, the brooding Lady of the Stag, the fretful Pike and the concerned Flora. He trailed a hand along the walls, thinking, trying not to think, trying to make himself a blank into which only one purpose could be placed. Hover paced behind him, and Simon found his presence comforting.

How long is it, he thought, *since I last saw my parents?* All that had happened since then flashed through his mind: the shadowsnake guarding the spheres, Raven and the Flames, Mithras, Giles Cuthbertson, the hunting horn, Francis Weston's house, that final race to the clearing, coming through the tear in reality here, to this place. Was it even real? What *was* real? He couldn't hold on to anything in his mind. Everything seemed to be shifting.

As if knowing he was upset, Hover put a hand on Simon's shoulder. Simon touched it appreciatively. It felt so good simply to have something – someone, if that's what Hover could be called – there who couldn't talk, couldn't worry, but simply offered companionship.

When he'd cleared his mind a little, he shone his torch around the cavern he was in. It was very similar to all the others, complete with a small ledge in the wall. Except that above this one a picture was scratched into the rock. Wiping his eyes, Simon got up and went over to look at it more closely.

There were three interlocking circles, like the Venn diagrams he'd done at school. In the one on the top left was the symbol of the horns, as he'd seen on the skin-map. The circle on the right contained another, smaller circle. The one at the bottom had nothing in it.

Are these the worlds? he wondered. There was writing of some sort around the circles, but he couldn't make it out. At least, he assumed it was writing. It could just be a pattern, meaningless and uncanny.

He began to feel dizzy. *Is that it?* he wondered. *Are those the limits of the universe?* He felt a sudden shift in his mind. *Everything I know,* he thought, *is upset. Worlds within worlds within worlds. How can we ever know or understand what's really true?*

Hover came closer and the dim light that shone from him lit up the picture more clearly. He traced the circles with his fingers, pausing in the centre where the three interlinked.

Hover seemed to be trying to indicate something to Simon.

'What is it?' asked Simon.

Hover bent forwards, the unearthly silver light suffusing his face, his features drawn into a look of studied concentration. There was something of the bird-deer still in his eyes, something a little haughty and challenging. Simon felt a connection forming with Hover, as if meaning was emanating from him, and he could only just about grasp it. It was like whispers, far off, forming into barely recognisable sounds. *If I just concentrate hard enough*, thought Simon, *I can understand it . . . These are the secrets of the universe, the pieces that make up our worlds, and they are almost within my grasp . . .*

He saw a woman, ancient but beautiful, and she was shining with light, and the light was now two women, of silver and gold, and now she also became a third woman, who was dark, and a snake came from her, and she was everything . . . It was beautiful, and he felt, looking into the woman's eyes, that he was staring into the origins of time and space.

There were footsteps outside in the passageway, and suddenly the chamber filled with the glow of a flaming torch.

The connection between him and Hover snapped, and Simon turned to see Flora and Pike. Hover moved protectively in front of Simon.

'We were worried about you,' said Flora, pushing past Hover and grabbing Simon in a big hug, which Simon returned. Pike came further in.

'Don't worry, I'm not doing a runner,' said Simon. 'How could I?'

'What are those?' asked Flora, pointing at the picture.

Simon shrugged. 'I don't know. I just found them.'

'It's the three worlds,' said Pike. 'And in the centre, where they meet, is the abode of the Threefold Goddess. Or so they say, anyway.'

'Are there more worlds?' asked Flora. 'I mean, I was pretty surprised to find out that this world – the one we're in – actually, like, exists and everything, but I have read a bit about quantum physics and stuff, about the possibility of many alternate universes, but just three worlds seems a bit . . . well, like not very much.'

'I don't know what you're talking about,' said Pike. 'I don't know what quantum . . . quantum physics means. These are the three worlds, and this is how it's always been. As far as I know, anyway,' he added thoughtfully.

'What's outside them?' asked Simon. 'I mean, what are they in?'

Pike looked troubled. 'The void, of course,' he said. 'They're inside nothing. Outside of the worlds is nothing, and inside are the three worlds, and they're linked by the Way.' He turned to the markings on the wall. 'This is the Silver Kingdom, shown by the horns — the horns of the crescent moon. That's the Golden Realm, and its symbol is the circle of the sun.'

'Mithras,' said Simon, 'was worshipped by the Romans as a sun god.'

'Yes, he's important in the Golden Realm. Very.'

'And the third?' said Simon.

'You,' replied Pike. 'It's you.'

'What do you call us?'

Again, Pike looked surprised. 'The place in-between,' he said. 'Didn't you know?'

The place in-between, thought Simon. *That's all we are. No name, no sign, just the place in-between.* The vast emptiness of it struck him and he held tightly on to the ledge.

'We don't even have a proper name?' he said slowly.

'I think you did once,' said Pike, a little flippantly, 'but it's been forgotten.' Pike stopped, noticing Simon's expression.

Flora, too, was gazing fiercely at him. 'So you didn't even have a reason to visit us?'

Pike shrugged. 'There just wasn't much point. People only went to take the Blessed Ones, and then —'

'So wait. Hold on,' said Simon. 'Tell me about these Blessed Ones.'

'The ones not wanted by their siblings are taken by the king.'

'Why?'

'To prolong his life, of course. How else do you think he's stayed king for so long?'

Simon clenched his fists. 'And you could do this because?'

'There was a treaty. Between King Selenus of the Kingdom, and Queen Helena of the Realm. Before the treaty, he used to take them whenever he wanted. I think there are stories in your world, aren't there, about children vanishing? Sometimes people from the three worlds intermingled. My mother is from the Golden Realm. Once there was a herald from the Golden Realm, who left a son in your world, by a woman he loved there. The son was beautiful, bright and golden, and the Broken King took him without warning, and used him, and killed him.

'The Realm threatened war unless he stopped his

practice. He refused, and so it was agreed that he would only take two people each one of your years if he was called, and he'd have to provide a way for the siblings to get them back if they desired. But none succeeded.'

'So we're the first?' said Simon.

Flora interjected. 'And your king preyed on us before that? For how long?'

'Time moves differently here. It's hard to tell.'

'Make a guess,' said Flora, through gritted teeth.

'Well, it was a long time before I was born. In my great-grandfather's time, perhaps. I remember him writing something down, drawing pictures of some strange clothes you used to wear, funny things around your necks . . .' He made a sign with his finger, drawing a wide circle around his neck.

'Ruffs?' said Simon sharply.

'That's the one! We did think that was funny. What on earth are they for?'

'Like, Elizabethan ruffs? Big white starchy things around your neck?'

'Yes – why in the name of the crescent would anybody want to wear something like that?'

'To keep their clothes clean, I think,' said Flora automatically.

Five hundred years, thought Simon. *For five hundred of our years the Broken King's taken children from us, and used them to keep him young. And how many before that treaty? Nobody asked us. They don't even bother with a name for us.*

In a blinding rage he punched the wall. The pain cracked through him and when, befuddled, he looked at his knuckles, he saw that the skin had come off them and he was bleeding. He watched the tiny drop of scarlet blood form, and sucked at it.

And it's not even my fault, he thought. *They made me do it.*

Helped me do it, came another voice in his mind.

Pike went to Simon. 'I . . . I'm sorry, I didn't . . .'

But Simon just turned away, staring at the symbols and wishing he were back in the place in-between. *Earth*, he thought. *It's called Earth. And I live there with millions of other people and we got along quite happily without knowing about these other worlds. The Realm and the Kingdom. Named as if they were the only ones.*

He shrugged Flora's comforting hand off his shoulder, and put his forehead to the cold stone, wishing for blackness.

Chapter Thirteen

THE

FLYING MAN

'WE DON'T HAVE any choice, do we?' said Simon to Flora. The silver sun had risen and set twice since Simon had seen the circles on the wall. Though they were confined to the temple cave complex, there was enough space to roam around in and not meet anyone, and Simon had been spending a lot of time thinking. They were in the chamber where the circles were. Hover was sitting with his back to the wall, his eyes blank. Pike was in another part of the temple cave, busy with the Lady of the Stag, planning the attack. Simon felt at peace there, in the cave of the circles. Or at least, as he contemplated the worlds and the insignificance of his own in relation to the others, he felt in less turmoil.

'Not really,' said Flora, who was examining the circles on the wall carefully.

'It's just so . . .'

'Horrible?' cut in Flora.

Three worlds, he thought, *and at the centre, where they touch – what is there? The Threefold Goddess, Pike said. But what if there's nothing? A blackness. A void. Nothing comes from nothing . . .*

'Worse things happen in our world,' said Flora, 'than the king taking children. Child soldiers . . . Genocide . . .'

'But it's so . . . inhuman!' cried out Simon, turning and fixing her with his eyes.

'I guess they're not really like us though, are they?' sighed Flora. 'They've got some other set of rules. We can't ever truly hope to understand them. Maybe they're not even the same species as us.'

'They're always deadly, aren't they?' said Simon. 'Fairies. They're beautiful and frightening and they'll kill you for no reason. Ha! Tinkerbell!'

'They're not fairies, though, are they?'

'Well,' said Simon, defeated, 'you know what I mean. Elves. Glamorous otherworldly beings. Whatever.'

The Lady of the Stag entered. 'We've had a message,' she said. 'It's time to get ready.'

She led them out, walking with swift purpose, into the main chamber where Pike was waiting.

'The ceremony starts tomorrow morning,' said Lavinia, 'so we have to get out of the city now, whilst it's dark, and into position behind the rocks near the standing stone.'

It was a strange procession that left the temple cave complex. The Lady of the Stag went first, disguised as a farmer's wife, with Flora as her daughter. She would go out by a way she knew well, near the gate of Eurus, where there was an empty house that had a cellar that led out under the walls. From there they would take the route under a line of trees that led to the rocks and the standing stone.

To avoid being seen together, they would go different ways. Pike, Simon and Hover would go to a secret gap in the wall in the Blindings near the gate of Notus, but, though the guards were not aware of it, the area was often watched. And after they'd got through, they would have to make their way across open country.

Simon said goodbye to Flora. 'This could be it.'

Flora nodded abruptly in response. 'See you

there,' she said, hiding her feelings. As she and the lady left, Simon felt a deep pang of affection for Flora. *I* will *see you there*, he thought.

Pike swaddled himself up in a cloak, and gave one to Simon before going out through the hidden entrance into the alleyway. Simon was glad of Hover's presence. The strange, silent being moved not quite like a robot, but there was definitely something mechanical about him.

Pike went ahead with surefooted ease. The moon was covered with clouds, though its faint reddish light seeped out. They'd muffled up Hover so tightly that his silver features were mostly obscured. If stopped, they would say he was dangerously ill with the black spot, and they were taking him to a wise man for a cure, and they'd have to hope that nobody would dare to go near him. Fear of the black spot would send most scuttling away.

Whenever they heard what might be footsteps, Pike kept them pressed back in the shadows. Sometimes a hooded, cloaked figure would slip by, bent on its own mysterious business, as keen to remain hidden as they were. Sometimes a light would appear in a house above them, and Simon would see a face, illuminated and still, before the light was extinguished. The portraits of the king loomed unexpectedly, causing Simon to start in fear. They pressed on down the cobbled streets.

Sometimes Simon thought a shadow shivered and rushed off. He remembered the royal hounds, with their scales and feathers and teeth and slavering jaws and staring red eyes.

He focused on Pike's figure, his outline dim in the gloom. If he reached out, he would be able to touch him, and he kept his pace the same as Pike's. He didn't have to look behind to know that Hover was there, but felt him. The hunting horn nuzzled into his bicep, and that too gave off a curious energy. He was half glad he hadn't had to use it again. And terrified of using it on the king.

Don't be afraid, thought Simon. *Don't. You'll get through it.*

As they moved stealthily along the narrow, twisting streets, his mind focused itself into something sharp.

Suddenly Pike crouched and hissed at them, and both Simon and Hover dropped to the ground.

Inching up towards Pike, Simon peered over his shoulder. There, in a little patch of torchlight, were two guards, walking in a desultory manner up and down the path.

'They're in the way,' whispered Pike.

The soldiers were big and beefy, and carried two bright silver torches. They were talking in ordinary voices.

'. . . listen to this, right, Griff, and Big Mully said she'd punch him halfway to the Southern Marches. And old Pubbles says, "Go on, then". And she does! Knocks him right to the door!"

The other guard laughed. 'Would have loved to see the look on his face, Old Jem.' Jem slapped Griff on the back, and they had another hearty laugh about Big Mully punching the lights out of Pubbles.

Pike was as still as a hare in its form. Simon couldn't see Hover. He himself was biting his lip. The guards looked like they were about to move on.

Simon almost sighed with relief. But somebody must have done something, because one of the guards – Griff, Simon thought – said, 'Hey, what's that?'

Griff turned towards where the three were crouching, and started pacing towards them, torch held aloft. Simon could see his bruiserish face and a piggy kind of look in his eyes. Old Jem whistled a low, sad tune, singing the occasional word.

Griff approached. 'Looks like someone's there . . .' His torch flared and lit up the three of them. They all stiffened. 'Jem! Over here! Look – we got three pups, out after curfew.'

Jem, laughing to himself, began to totter over.

Before Pike and Simon could say or do anything, Hover stood up and uncovered himself. He was starting to glimmer a little, noticed Simon.

'Pretty little thing,' leered Jem. 'Maybe I'll take you back to the guardhouse. It's a slow night.'

'I saw her first,' protested Griff.

Slowly, elegantly, Hover stepped forwards and moved between the two guards.

'It's not a girl,' exclaimed Griff, sounding puzzled.

'We'll have to wait and see, won't we,' scoffed Jem.

Griff pulled Pike up by the scruff of his neck. Simon, frightened, but ready to defend him if he could, stood up too.

'Two rats we've got here. Though you don't look much like your ordinary rat,' sneered the guard at Pike. Pike stayed limp. 'You look like you've been palace bred. Why aren't you safe at home with your nurse, knightling?'

Pike said nothing.

'You,' continued the guard, indicating Simon, 'I don't know what to make of you.' Something seemed to occur to him, as he called over his shoulder to his companion. 'Here.' Jem was circling Hover with a horrible leer on his face. 'What was it the princess said we should look out for? A boy and a girl?'

'That's not these,' said Jem. 'This one's definitely not a girl.'

'Let's round them up anyway,' said Griff, and grabbed Simon by his arm.

Nobody expected what happened next.

Hover, his shimmering light getting brighter, started to grow again, into someone much taller.

But what was even more surprising was that out of his back sprouted two huge wings, bright like the tail feathers of a peacock, which he shook out and beat.

Griff dropped Simon in his astonishment. Hover jumped up into the air and swooped down on to Old Jem, taking him out with a well-timed kick to the chin, and then, spinning round in mid-air so fast that Simon felt the breeze on his face, knocked Griff in the stomach. Griff stumbled backwards and fell, an astonished look replacing the pigginess in his eyes.

As he slumped to the ground, Simon heard Griff whisper, 'The flying man . . . It's the coming of the end . . .'

Then he passed out.

'Quick,' whispered Pike, 'before their friends come.'

'What did he mean?' asked Simon.

Hover's wings retracted, and he shrank back to his usual human size, joining Pike as the three of them ran across the street to the jumble of buildings on the other side.

'Tell you later,' said Pike. 'Let's get out first.'

There was a low and crumbling house, with a tiny alleyway next to it. Above them the black city wall rose up. 'Here,' said Pike, and indicated a shrub growing out of the wall. 'Go on, quickly!'

Simon, puzzled, went to the shrub, tugged at it, and was surprised to find that it sprang aside and revealed a hole just large enough for him to go through. Simon looked for a split second at Pike, who waved him on, and then, gritting his teeth, plunged in.

It was dark, and for a moment – feeling nothing but wall on either side of him, and seeing nothing ahead – he panicked. He crept on, inch by inch, the stone grazing his hands. On and on he went. *How can the wall be this thick?* he thought.

He suddenly felt the night breeze on his face, and the path slope downwards, and he came out into the air, gulped some into his lungs, and tumbled down into the ditch that ran along the bottom of the wall. It was a little muddy and he hoped it was nothing worse than that.

He looked out over the plain. He could make out the shapes of trees, but not much else. The reddish moon was high. He heard scuffling behind him, then Hover elegantly glided down to land beside him, smiling obscurely. A few seconds later, Pike followed, puffing a little.

'Now comes the hardest bit,' he said in a soft tone. 'Keep low, and keep to what cover you can find.'

They scrambled up the other side of the ditch, and then, almost on their hands and knees, went straight for a clump of bushes about twenty paces away. This was the most exposed part. Any guard looking down from the city wall would be able to see them and reach them with an arrow. Simon looked up at the cloudy sky and thanked the gods – whoever they were. *The Threefold Goddess*, he thought.

Reaching the low, springy, prickly bushes, Simon was beginning to feel excited. The cool night air was instilling energy into him. The simple thrill of being outside after so long cooped up in those dark and dank caves was filling his blood.

They zigzagged across to a tree surrounded by bushes, and crouched down behind them. They were now a hundred paces or so away from the ditch, and they could see no movement on the battlements of the wall. Simon took in the city as they caught their breath. In the dark it was even more ominous. The towers of the palace could just about be seen, outlined in reddish light, and he imagined the king pacing around his chamber, laughing, his dwarf and his giant beside him. *And my sister with them too*, he thought, and courage firmed his heart.

'To the standing stone,' said Pike, and on they went.

Chapter Fourteen

THE CEREMONY

OF SUNDERING

JOHNNY WAS PROWLING around the edges of the sheer black walls that hemmed in the Blessed Ones. Occasionally he would touch them, trying to find a gap. Anna was quietly playing with a bit of string, winding it round and round her fingers, letting the light play on her silver hands. She had taken off her golden coronet, and it lay, discarded, by her side.

'We need to find a way out of here,' Johnny said.

'How?' said Anna, looking up from her desultory game. 'Bruin never speaks to us any more, Malek has never spoken to us, and those horrible monkeys . . .'

She shuddered at the thought of the creatures. 'We never get to talk to anyone else, anyway,' said Anna. 'Andaria just stares at us . . . I don't like her. I don't like any of them. I want Bertie!' Bertie was her purple and orange stuffed dog. She really wanted her mother and father, but she didn't want to say that in front of Johnny.

'How long have we been here?' said Johnny.

'Ages and ages and ages.' It was longer than Anna had ever spent in one place that wasn't at home. It was longer than having to wait for Christmas. 'The days . . . are always the same.' In the time she'd been there, sometimes the king wouldn't even ask to see them, and they'd be left in their prison all day and night. Sometimes food and drink would appear; sometimes they would not. The troubling thing was that you would never know when the king would call. It made them anxious, jittery. Anna jumped at shadows, at clouds passing over the sun. Her dreams were full of hands clutching at her.

'I heard them talking,' said Johnny. 'Something about a ceremony . . .'

'Stupid ceremonies. And you were stupid at the last one,' said Anna, more unkindly than she meant. Cowed a little by her own forwardness, she turned and continued to play with her string.

'I just thought we might be able to try something . . .'

'I'm playing,' said Anna, ignoring him. 'And you're not allowed to play with me.'

'Oh God,' replied Johnny, clenching his fists together. 'Anything is better than this . . .'

'Humph,' said Anna, relenting. 'Outside, maybe there's lots of food. I wish they had orange juice.'

'Maybe there's some kind of resistance to his rule?' said Johnny vehemently. 'Maybe there are whole villages, towns, cities out there, all waiting for their chance . . . I hear them talk about the Southern Marches, the ports of Notus and Boreas – there's a whole country out there, and beyond that – what? Is it like our world? Maybe this is just one country in a whole planet of countries, and we can escape and the other peoples could bring us back home,' said Johnny, and shivered, wondering who 'the other peoples' might be.

He hadn't had a chance to put on any clothes when he was taken. Not even his leather jacket. He'd been in his boxer shorts. They'd given him these . . . robes, he supposed they were. He glanced at his reflection in the black wall, and thought he looked like he was in a play, with his silver cheek and flowing dress.

He remembered the white, grinning face that he'd thought was a hallucination. He'd moaned at it, turned over, put his head in his hands. It was just a symptom of his withdrawal.

But the rushing, the snatching, that had all seemed so real. And when he'd woken up – expecting his room with his Union Jack duvet, the window open to the summer air, the smell of cooking rising up from downstairs, the sound of Flora stomping around the house – he'd been on his back in this room.

And then later – he didn't know how long it had been – Anna had appeared, frightened and weeping.

It had all seemed like a terrible dream. *And still*, he thought, as he paced the confines of their prison once more, *I haven't woken up.*

Oh no, thought Selena groggily as she woke. *Today is the day of the Ceremony of Sundering.* She sat up quickly. *Why didn't Clara wake me?* Then she remembered the past couple of days, and what had happened with the Knight of the Swan, and paused as she put her feet on the thick fur rug by her bed. Her pet hound snuffled, and padded over to lick her leg. She ruffled his head.

Someone was in her room – a shadow by the doorway. Was that a sword? She reached for her scabbard, and the shadow resolved itself into Clara, who was holding a washbasin that she was bringing to the side of her bed. It steamed, and Selena could smell the welcoming tang of fresh herbs.

'Are you well?' asked Clara timidly.

'Yes, of course,' snapped Selena. Then, a little more kindly, 'I'll dress myself this morning, thank you. And you're late.'

As soon as Clara had gone, Selena bent to sniff the water to check it for anything strange; her pet hound padded over and eyed it critically, then slunk off. *It's fine*, thought Selena. *This is ridiculous. I'm seeing death everywhere.*

She thought back to what had happened at the steward's house. They'd captured the Knight of the Swan. This was bad, as it must have been noticed by now. But was she still being watched?

Every step I take, she thought, as she tied herself into a long ceremonial gown – heavy, dark green, and embroidered with images of the moon – *is fraught with danger.*

The plan will have to go ahead today, she thought as she placed on her head the tiara that had one single emerald at the centre of it. *And I can't do anything to help it. It's down to them.* She clipped on her sword belt, and stuck her sword into her scabbard. *Will they be able to do it?*

The Lady of the Stag I don't doubt, she thought, stepping through the door into the busy corridors. The black walls on either side reflected her as she walked. Two servants, in their discreet black clothes, stopped and bowed to her. She gave them the curtest of replies as she swept past, her dress billowing behind her.

I know Pike's provenance, she reflected. *The Knight of the Shark was a good man, and he didn't have to die. But the other two . . . Simon Goldhawk and Flora Williamson. They completed the three tasks, sure. But are they ready for the final challenge?*

When she reached the central throne room, she found the king pacing up and down in front of his huge silver throne. The Blessed Ones, in simple white gowns, were tied to a post and guarded by the two little unnamed creatures, who jumped up and down and snickered when she came in. The king's scarlet robe was long, and his horns had been painted red. His face was covered in white powder, and he grinned, revealing a red tongue poking between white teeth.

'Father,' she said.

'News,' he replied. 'Andaria has brought news. Strange things happening on the Southern Marches . . .'

'What, Father? What did she find?'

He paused. 'Golden flashes. Appearances in dreams. The rustle of wings. They see things from the Realm, out there.'

'The visions of peasants, Father.'

'I hear of the man who flies, too,' continued the king, pacing up and down.

A whisper went round the room between the courtiers. *The man who flies. The harbinger of ruin.*

'But that is just a story,' said Selena.

'I am not at all certain,' he replied, 'if it is just a story. Am I not a story, in the place in-between? They think I am a figment of imagination – until I take their children. The winged man . . . It seems as if . . . the *Realm* is plotting . . . They sent avatars to help the brats . . . What more might they do?'

'You know they can't get through, Father. The Way is closed. It's nothing.'

'There are other ways . . . And the Knight of the Swan has vanished too. Has he deserted me?'

Careful, thought Selena. *Don't give anything away.*

'He is out somewhere on your mission, hunting

for the two from the place in in-between.'

'Yes,' said the king grandly. 'He is out on his quest for me, looking for those bratlings . . .'

Anna pricked her ears up at that. She tried to hear what was going on over the noise of the monkey-things, but couldn't. The little creatures chattered their teeth and tickled each other with a long feather they'd found somewhere. One of them poked at her nose with it, and she sneezed.

The clock in the wall above the door slid towards five hours after dawn, and a gentle chiming filled the air.

'So,' the king announced, 'it is time for the ceremony.' He clicked his fingers, and the two chattering creatures unhooked the chains of the Blessed Ones and led them over to the king. Bruin and Malek, never far away, materialised from somewhere and took their places on either side of the king. They too were dressed in red, both in some kind of tough-looking material. Malek stared stonily ahead, whilst Bruin's gentle eyes seemed always to be looking somewhere else.

'We praise the Day of Sundering!' shouted the king.

'We praise the Day of Sundering,' replied all in

the room. Selena noted the bright colours of the armour, the flounces of the dresses, the banners and the helmets with their animal crests. Andaria slid forward and strode beside the king. She looked pleased with herself, her mouth twisted in a sly grin.

Followed by his retainers, the king – his shadow buzzing around him – stepped out and through the palace and the city, on his way to the standing stone.

Where Simon and Flora will be waiting for you, thought Selena. *And I wish them luck.* For a moment, the curve of his neck as he straightened himself reminded her of the father she'd known when she was little, and though she felt a pang of sorrow and love as she saw her father step through the door, she crushed it down until it was as tight and small as a pebble. His horns cast a shadow on the ground as he left, and the two little creatures danced through it.

Pike was keeping watch, peering out behind the rocks by the standing stone, towards the city across the vast plain. Simon was reminded of when they'd arrived, and he and Flora had been taken by the carter. *What happened to him?* he wondered, feeling a little bit guilty. He'd been alive when they left him, at least.

The silver sun was reaching up across the sky, and a few clouds flitted across, their shadows making darker patches on the already dark plain. The trees with their black bark and purpleish leaves seemed threatening and full of warnings. The dawn here was much more sudden than on Earth; it seemed for a moment as if the whole world were made of silver, and when Simon saw it as he kept watch, he gasped in wonder.

Flora was fretting, tapping her fingers on the sheath of the sunsword. The Lady of the Stag was resting, gazing out across the plain towards the city. They'd had an easier journey, and hadn't been stopped or questioned. They'd already had an hour or so of rough sleep on the rocky ground, underneath the reddish moon, taking it in turns to keep watch, when Simon, Pike and Hover had arrived.

The Lady of the Stag had provided hot drinks and food, and Simon concentrated on his breakfast. The drink was spicy and sour at the same time; the bread was flat and hard but delicious, with a deep, bitter flavour he'd never tasted before.

Simon shifted the hunting horn from its place at his side, and balanced it on his knees. *It is so black*, he thought. *And so powerful.*

'How do I control it?' he asked Lavinia.

'There are many notes,' she replied. 'You have to feel its power and direct it, as if you were directing a stream of water with a tap. There are notes which can break apart rocks. But when it comes to the king's shadow, you will need to blow the note of death.'

'How will I know the note?' asked Simon. 'And will it . . . kill him?'

'You will know,' answered the lady. 'And yes, it will allow him to be killed.'

I don't know if I could cause someone to be killed, thought Simon. *But then, is he really a person? He is a monster . . .*

Hover stood silent and still, the same calm, pure expression on his face.

'The king will go by himself to kneel and pray at the standing stone,' said Lavinia briskly, noticing the faraway look in Simon's eyes. 'When he does that, we attack. We won't have much time, as he's bound to have a magehawk with him, which will immediately go back to the city for reinforcements. Once Pike and I have disabled the guards – Andaria, Bruin and Malek – Flora and Simon – you're on.'

'What . . . what exactly do we have to do?' said Flora, who was feeling a little anxious.

'The sunsword is the only blade that can slice

through the king's protective shadow, and the horn's blast will keep the shadow torn apart. Then Flora – you deliver the killing stroke with the sunsword.'

To cover up his agitation, Simon asked, 'What did the guard mean? About the flying man?'

'The beginning of the end? Oh, it's just an old story,' said Pike casually.

'What's that?' said Lavinia.

'When we came out into the city,' said Simon, 'Hover turned into something else. Well, he grew wings. The guard who saw it called it the beginning of the end.'

'Did he now?' said Lavinia, looking at Hover. 'I can well believe it . . . I told you there was something more to this than work from the Realm.'

'But why did the guard say that?'

'It's just a silly story,' said Pike. 'Something the country folk tell their children. He must have grown up in a village beyond the forest and come into the town to be on the king's guard. They went rounding up all the big men a few years ago.'

'I know it,' said Lavinia. 'I had a nurse from one of the villages up by the Towers of Boreas, near the White mountains . . .' She smiled. 'There's a tune, as well.' She sang, in a soft alto.

'When man has wings, the end begins
When man can fly, the worlds shall die.'

The tune was gentle, at odds with the words. When she finished, there was silence, and the wind rustled through their small encampment. 'It's a rhyme, nothing more.'

That's what I thought about calling the Broken King, thought Simon, *and see what happened.* He looked at Hover with renewed interest.

'They're coming,' said Pike.

The king was being pulled in an open carriage. Bruin the giant and Malek the dwarf were seated on either side of him. Andaria was proudly astride the lead horse. Simon could see the king's red robe, bright against the blackness of the city's towers. The slow, horned horses pulling him made steady progress. Around the carriage were guards, with royal hounds pulling at leashes. And behind them – his heart leaped. There were two white-robed people that must be . . .

As the carriage drew nearer, he saw with clarity. Anna was huddled up in a corner. Johnny was sitting, clutching his knees, looking troubled.

The carriage halted before the standing stone. The king, in his red finery, his protective shadow buzzing around him, stepped down from it and called to the Blessed Ones to follow him – something that wasn't necessary, as the two little chattering creatures pulled on their silver chains and they had no choice but to move. A magehawk preened itself on the king's carriage. The Blessed Ones tumbled out on to the ground and stood, shakily.

The Lady of the Stag was keeping very still, peering through a crack in the rocks; Pike, Simon and Flora were in a row, ready to jump out; Hover was simply standing inert, hidden from the king and his companions behind a large rock.

There were only four guards, and all were carrying weapons. Bruin and Malek were unarmed. Andaria, aloof and unconcerned, leaned against the carriage.

'Who is Andaria?' Simon whispered.

'Nobody knows where she came from,' answered Lavinia. 'She appeared one day and offered herself to the king's service. She said she comes from somewhere far beyond the Bay of Zephyrus, over the seas – a place of forests, where the Kingdom does not reach.'

'So there are places he doesn't rule in this world?'

'Far and barren, and few dwell there. His pets

come from some country over the sea – they washed up on the beach, clutching a piece of mast. They cannot speak, at least they cannot make sounds we understand, so we cannot tell where they are from.'

Flora was beginning to sweat. She watched the king as he raised his hands into the air in benediction, and then threw himself, prostrate, at the foot of the standing stone, pulling the Blessed Ones with him. She watched his shadow, buzzing around him, wondering how thick it was, if cutting it would hurt him . . .

Simon thought about the ancient, cruel, mad king. He found the idea of harming him immensely troubling, yet at the same time he could not wait to bring him low. How many centuries of evil had burned in his mind?

Andaria's snow-white horned horse whinnied and stamped its feet, chinking its bridle. Simon looked at her more closely. She was dressed all in dark green, and she had a bow slung over her back, with a quiver of arrows jutting out from behind it.

The king was still chanting. It was hot, the silver sun beating down. The black trees made Simon feel disoriented. He had a sudden rush of longing for the greens and golds of the Sussex countryside. The king released the chains, and the Blessed Ones stepped back towards the cart. Anna whimpered, and Johnny stroked her hair.

Turning to the standing stone, the king bowed, the horses snorted, and the small band of rebels readied themselves.

Now's the moment, thought Simon. *I'm ready for it.* He pulled all his strength into him, and focused his mind on to one point: the king. *Put him out of action, rescue Anna, then go home. Home.*

Flora was standing to his right, and she was calm, her hand resting lightly on the sunsword's hilt. Her nostrils were slightly flared. Their eyes met, and he felt an electric sense of possibility spark between the two of them. *We are together now, in life or death,* thought Simon. He grasped Flora's hand, and she returned the pressure. This was it. Lavinia was giving the signal. One . . . two . . .

Then, just as they were about to charge into the open, Hover moved. The Lady of the Stag held back Simon and Flora. Hover slowly paced out from where he'd been hiding, stepping daintily, fluttering his eyelids.

'What is he doing?' breathed the Lady of the Stag.

Anna was the first to notice the strange silver being.

She couldn't help herself exclaiming, then squealing with delight. *That's my Anna*, thought Simon.

'A spaceman!' called Anna.

The guards all levelled their weapons at Hover, but he stood, unconcerned, in the middle of their encircling spears.

The king noticed something was going on and sat up from his prayer. Seeing Hover, he stood and approached him. The guards fell back. Hover didn't move. The king looked Hover up and down, slowly inspecting him. Then he pulled a long silver blade from his horn, and picked his fingernails with it.

'Say something,' said the king, casually.

Hover didn't.

'What are you, then?' continued the king. 'A present from my knights? From my people? Who sent you?' He opened his arms wide, and swished from side to side. 'I shall reward whoever sent this most beautiful creature. Have you come to sing my praises on the Day of Sundering? Eh?' He stalked around Hover, peering at him from all angles. 'I don't recognise you, or what you are, at all. Has one of my knights made you? Where are they all anyway?'

'They remain in the city, your majesty,' Bruin said, shifting his bulk.

The king experimentally touched Hover's shoulder. Nothing happened, though his shadow fizzed a little.

'This thing is not of interest,' said the king, sighing. 'Destroy it. All things like this are to be destroyed. Whatever they are. Make a note of it.' He went back to the standing stone and kneeled.

A guard aimed a blow at Hover, and his spear glanced off him.

Then two things happened at once.

The first was that a rider, mounted on one horned horse and leading another, came galloping down the road from the city towards them.

The second was that Hover started to shapeshift once more.

Nearer and nearer came the horned horses, the rider's shouts filling the air. There was confusion amongst the guards, who scrambled away from Hover. The king himself jumped to his feet once more.

The horned horses' hooves thundered on the black road.

Hover wasn't just shifting, he was growing. Beneath him sprouted four spindly legs, and then a body, and then wings on either side of it; then he rose up in the air until it was clear that he was sitting astride a bird-deer. *Just like the messengers I first met,* thought Simon. *But silver, not gold.*

'What is this?' shouted the king. The guards were bristling with their spears. Andaria had an arrow straining at her bowstring. Bruin and Malek were at the king's side, both ready to fight.

The horned horses pounded ever closer.

The king's face was contorted, his red mouth wide in rage. 'You dare,' he said, 'to enter my kingdom?'

Hover smiled, bowed, and spoke. Like the messengers he did not speak with his mouth, yet somehow everyone there heard the words in their minds.

'It has been witnessed,' said Hover. 'A guard of the Broken King has attacked an emissary of the Golden Realm without provocation. This is legal justification for war.'

The king yelled and threw a dagger at Hover; it clattered uselessly to the rocky ground.

Hover shimmered, flickered, bowed again, and said, 'We are massing on your borders. Send us your ambassador. We shall meet him at the port of Notus. Until then.'

He bowed once more, then the bird-deer shook its

wings out, and Hover flew away. Andaria ran after him and shot an arrow, but he was out of reach, and soon he had gone completely.

Simon felt absolutely betrayed. *We should do it now,* he thought. *Before this war starts. We were just pawns. Helping us wasn't the real reason at all for their actions. They just wanted me to carry Hover into the Kingdom to declare war.*

'Let's do it now!' he whispered to Flora. 'Let's just go. We can do it, the two of us, whilst they're all confused.'

Flora looked at him and he knew she understood him.

'Before all this starts . . .'

But as he pushed himself off the rock and was about to go out into the open, the horned horses from the city arrived.

The rider was helmeted, and on the other horse was a little bundle of clothes.

'Sire! I have a prize for you!' shouted the rider.

The king's face softened. He extended a hand gracefully. 'What is it?'

The rider took off his helmet, and held it under his arm.

Simon's heart sank.

The king repeated his question. 'What is the prize, Knight of the Swan?'

He'd escaped. The Lady of the Stag looked terrified.

'We can't attack now – he's too powerful!' Pike was clutching his temples.

Flora had her hands clamped over her mouth; Simon was poised. 'Don't move, any of you,' he hissed.

'A brave prize, indeed,' continued the knight. He indicated the horned horse he was leading, and the bundle tied to it.

'What is it, my loyal knight? You bring me happiness in a time of great sadness!'

And with a sickening lurch, Simon realised that the little bundle of clothes on the saddle of the other horse was a person. It moved, and made a noise halfway between a splutter and a shriek.

'The greatest prize of all, my liege. The greatest traitor of all. Your daughter. I bring you the renegade princess!'

Chapter Fifteen

RETREAT
TO THE FOREST

'HOW DID HE escape?' Furious, the Lady of the Stag rounded on Scarlet, Eagret and the others who'd been left to guard the Knight of the Swan. Simon was hanging back in the entrance to the cave chamber where they were gathered. Flora was quietly grim; Pike was nowhere to be seen.

Eagret said, 'I don't know. It happened so fast.'

'Eagret! There were three of you! On him, at all times! He was bound hand and foot! And gagged!'

This is all wrong, thought Simon. *I'll never rescue Anna now. And Hover! All that time, an emissary of the Realm! He must have been programmed to declare war if it was possible . . . And that's what the princess wanted, too, wasn't it? Admittedly, she wanted her father to attack them first, but they don't care about us at all! We're nothing to them!* He felt small and insignificant and hurt, and went to Flora and wrapped her in his arms.

They'd waited till the king had gone into the city, and snuck back via their separate routes. They'd found the inhabitants of the temple cave complex banded together in the main chamber.

Scarlet stepped forwards. 'What she says is true. It happened too fast to do anything. One minute, we were watching him, the next, there was a flash, a blur, and we were knocked over and left helpless. I saw him . . .' she continued sniffily. 'He moved faster than any of us. I couldn't stop him. Before I could open my mouth to even say anything – *bang*, he'd gone.'

They hung their heads, and Lavinia fumed. Simon felt sorry for them.

Flora pushed him off and came back to her senses. 'But what are we going to do now?' she said.

Lavinia said, 'The king will order a Taking Apart for the princess. There's no doubt about it. And we are in terrible danger too. Who knows what the princess will say under torture?'

I trust her, thought Simon. *I know she won't give*

anything away. She cares too much. 'Well, there's only one thing for it,' he said quietly.

All eyes in the chamber turned to him. Flora nodded, slowly. She could guess what Simon was about to say.

'We have to rescue her.'

Lavinia lifted her chin. 'That means . . . showing ourselves. In public.'

'It's the only way,' said Simon. 'We storm the execution, take them by surprise, rescue Anna, Johnny and Selena, and flee.'

'I admire your courage,' said Lavinia. 'But it's mad.'

'Wait,' said Pike, appearing at the doorway of the chamber. He was standing there looking thoughtful, resting against the stone. 'He has a point. The king will send a well-guarded embassy down to the port of Notus to meet with emissaries of the Realm. There will only be relatively few guards left in the city. The people may turn a blind eye to us – they are already against Takings Apart, and so are most of the knights. Maybe this could be our chance!'

'But his guards are loyal to him.'

'He'll send the Knight of the Swan on the embassy,' said Pike. 'That leaves Andaria, Bruin, Malek, those horrible little monkey creatures, the royal hounds, and the remaining guards.'

'So quite a lot, then,' said Flora wearily.

'How many are we?' asked Simon.

'Look around,' said Lavinia.

From out of the shadows came maybe a dozen faces, all young, all frightened; even the three tall men that had carried them in were tense and worried.

'I see,' said Flora. 'We've got quite a task ahead of us . . .'

But we've done so much already, thought Simon. *Is this what I am meant to do? Am I meant to be a leader?* He felt things coming together in his heart, deep inside him.

'Now,' said Lavinia, addressing the chamber. 'Our king is mad. He has killed our relatives. He rules with tyranny and with fear. Our Silver Princess has been captured, and she is our only hope. We must rescue her, and topple the king to set this country right.' Her low, powerful voice resounded through the caves, and filled them with vibrations. She turned and addressed them directly. 'You two, Simon and Flora, have shown extraordinary courage, bravery and fearlessness in coming here. And now we must ready ourselves for the end. But the Silver Kingdom will always be thankful to you and will honour you and remember you among the stars.'

'Among the stars,' chorused the rebels, and both Simon and Flora felt a flush of pride.

'The first thing we have to do,' said Lavinia, 'is get out of here. The Knight of the Swan will tell – has probably already told – the king exactly where we are. So pack up everything you need and meet me in the Chamber of the Circles as soon as possible.'

Flora beckoned to Simon, and the two of them set off with their meagre belongings, along the dark, twisting corridors, to wait in the chamber. They hadn't had a chance to talk since they'd got back from the standing stone, and now, facing each other in the cool, damp silveriness, they found they could not say anything at all.

They didn't have to stay silent for long, though, as Pike came running in. He had two swords strapped over his back, was wearing armour, and carrying several bags. 'There's a couple of soldiers outside, sniffing around,' he gasped. 'I think they're on to us.'

He was followed quickly by the rest of the rebels, and finally by the Lady of the Stag herself.

'Why bring us here?' said Simon. He could see no way out.

'This is a temple, ancient and holy,' said Lavinia. 'And what all holy places have in common – especially if they are ancient – is this.'

She paced up to the picture of the three interlinked worlds, and with the tip of her sword, pushed at the place where they all connected.

Immediately there was a rumbling sound, and the stone began to draw back, revealing a black, empty space beyond. *Always darkness*, thought Simon.

'This will lead us to a safe place,' she said. 'Go in, and I'll close up behind.'

There were shouts and banging in the distance.

'They've found the brick at the entrance,' said Pike. 'Quickly!'

More shouts. The clanking of armour. Then darkness as they stepped into the tunnel. The shift was so fast that Simon couldn't tell where Flora was, or discern Pike in the gloom. Then, if it was possible, the darkness became thicker, which Simon guessed signalled the passage being closed. *I hope Lavinia made it*, thought Simon.

Then there was nothing to think about except how to keep going.

Simon kept his mind focused. One step in front of the other. Ahead – he couldn't tell how far – he could see a light that bobbed and wavered. *Whoever's leading us must be holding that*, he thought.

The tiny pinprick of light wobbled and shivered and Simon started to feel dizzy. His mind was jumping around from place to place. He tried to calm it. *One, two, one, two.* The words in his mind beat and beat. The other noises around him merged into one. He felt in his sack for his torch, and clicked it on. The beam lit up wet rock, and a dim figure ahead. He called out, 'Hello?' The beam fizzed and spluttered, and then went out. The darkness thickened. He dropped the torch, fumbled for it, couldn't find it. He called again.

An answer came back, from where or whom he could not tell. He tripped on something and caught himself on the side of the tunnel; it was cool and mossy, and he pulled his hand away quickly, fearing things that might lurk on the surface. Was that something skittering away?

There was a thick, furry taste in his mouth. As he plodded on, he kept thinking, *One foot, two foot*, and repeated it, a terrible mantra, until he wasn't sure if he would ever be able to forget the thudding and the monotony.

He thought it would never end. All sense of time,

all sense of place, had vanished, and he had become a machine. All he could do was walk, and walk for ever, blindly, graspingly, into the unknown.

With a sudden jolt, he came up against something bulky, which on closer inspection turned out to be Eagret.

'Sorry,' he said automatically. And then somebody bumped into him.

'We must stop meeting like this,' said Flora, and Simon marvelled at her ability to stay in good humour.

'All clear,' boomed a voice, and something clicked and rolled, and then there was light. The Lady of the Stag pushed past Simon, and light, glorious, beautiful light, and air – sweet air – spilled across his face, and he stepped out into a small, open cave. Beyond the cave's mouth he could see open ground, dark green vegetation and black forest, and it was all he could do not to rush out immediately. He found himself edging towards the entrance and it was only Eagret's arm that held him back.

'Don't – we don't know if it's safe,' murmured Eagret, and Simon pressed on as near as he dared, where he was soon joined by Flora, and the two of them sat, gazing out into the black forest, as delightedly as if they'd been back at home.

'I broke the mechanism that opens that tunnel from the cave,' the Lady of the Stag said, panting. 'They'll never find it. We're safe.'

For the moment, thought Simon. The glint of the sunsword, the weight of the hunting horn, the bulge of the shadow-spheres in his pocket, all reminded him of what was to come.

Standing up with Flora, they faced the others, with new, blazing courage in their hearts. He folded his arms and said, 'We need a plan.'

And everyone around him grasped hands, and took his, and he held Flora's. *We will do this*, he thought.

The wind blew through the cave, and outside the trees whispered, and he imagined they were calling to each other in approval.

Chapter Sixteen

THE TOWER
CRUMBLES

JOHNNY WAS ON edge, and more so than usual. He'd had terrible cravings in the night, and had woken to ghostly phantoms passing before his eyes. He knew something had happened during the day – he'd seen the Knight of the Swan processing up the road towards the palace, in front of the king, who was doing a strange sort of jig in his carriage. The princess was tied up next to him, looking bedraggled and ill.

His own daughter, Johnny had thought. *What is he going to do to her?*

The king hadn't troubled them, and Johnny

hadn't gone back to sleep. The servant who brought them food had told him what the Knight of the Swan had said. Now the silver sun was just below the left of the black towers that stood opposite the palace on the southern side of the square, and Johnny was watching the scene below him, as he always did, looking for some sign or means of escape.

Surely one of them could help us, he thought, as he watched a soldier marching along the square stop to hitch up his belt, a carter driving his meagre wares from the villages to the market, a magehawk flashing like shadow through the air, and a rider galloping up to the palace gates. A dark green cloak billowed out behind the rider. *It's her,* he thought, *Andaria, the green rider.*

There was a plume of black smoke rising into the air from somewhere in the city, larger than any that could come from a chimney, and he watched clouds of ash settle on the white statues below.

Anna stirred, and woke.

'I liked the princess,' said Anna. 'Is it true?'

'That she's been working against the king?' Johnny shrugged. 'I don't know. The Knight of the Swan may have his own motives for saying that. If only we'd known – if she'd given us some kind of signal, we could have got out of here.'

'How do you know she wants to help us?' asked Anna.

'She must do. She must.' Johnny clutched his head and shook it. Anna, frightened, shifted away. Johnny released himself and looked back at her. 'Don't be scared, Anna,' he said, adopting a gentle tone of voice that he'd often used with Flora. 'Come here.'

He held out his hand and Anna, sobbing, came to him and wept into his side. He stroked her head gently, whispering quietly to her, until the sun was fully up and the square below full of people.

'I don't like that rider,' said Johnny when she'd quietened down. 'Andaria. She frightens me.'

'Why?' said Anna. 'More than the king?'

'It's just her face . . .' said Johnny. 'It's like something's . . . missing in her eyes.'

'What are they going to do the princess?' said Anna. It had been bothering her. Selena was beautiful, and she never said anything unkind or did anything cruel to them. In fact, she seemed simply to ignore them. Which was better, Anna thought, than the Contraption. She shivered.

Johnny suspected what the king might be about to do, and said carelessly, 'There'll be a Taking Apart, of course.'

Anna started crying again.

'Oh, I'm sorry,' said Johnny, lightly, feeling guilty.

Anna sniffed and drew her hand across her face. 'I want to play,' she said quietly. 'And you're allowed to play with me.' Johnny was about to agree when the black barrier shimmered around them and opened suddenly, and in came the Knight of the Swan.

'You have a new companion,' said the knight. 'I wonder if you'll like her.'

Behind him marched two soldiers in black armour, and they held the arms of Princess Selena.

Her hair was plastered to her face, and there was a bruise on her cheek. She looked dully around the room. She was still in the dark green, embroidered ceremonial gown that she had put on for the Ceremony of Sundering. It dragged, incongruously, behind her.

The two soldiers released her, and she turned, composed, and thanked them for their troubles. They bowed, then as if remembering something, snapped to attention and pretended that she didn't exist.

'Good boys,' said the knight. 'Nobody is to pay any respect to a renegade princess.'

Princess Selena smiled, and bowed ironically to the knight. 'What pleasant chambers you have brought me to,' she said. 'And such interesting companions. May I have my lady, Clara?'

'You may not,' said the knight. His nostrils quivered. 'The time of your Taking Apart has been settled. It will be after the embassy returns.'

'Who leads the embassy?' said the princess.

'The king's most loyal servant,' replied the knight, indicating himself. 'We travel to the port of Notus this day. Our embassy will take two days; we then return and prepare for war. You will be the perfect sacrifice to start with – a warning to all those who fail to pay due obeisance to their king!' The knight's face was shivering with rage. His eyes were wide, his mouth compressed into a thin line. He glanced around the room, and his expression softened. 'The daughter of a king,' he said. 'I thought you were wonderful. But all this time you were nothing more than a vile, poisonous snake in the grass, waiting to pour your venom into our glorious monarch!'

The princess stood firm, consoling herself with the fact that at least there were other rebels out there. The Lady of the Stag, Pike, the children's siblings . . . They would find a way to bring down the king. She might die, but there were others. Her sisters, even . . . She thought of her half-sisters, kept far away, in a stronghold by the ocean in the jagged Castle of Eurus. She could barely remember when had she last seen them. They were unlikely to lead a revolution, she thought, kept fat and placid as they were.

The knight nodded briskly, and inclined his head slightly to the children, but not to Selena. 'Oh, and by the way,' he said. 'We found the temple cave.'

Selena momentarily twitched. 'What temple?' she said innocuously.

'You know very well what temple. And we burned it to the ground.'

So that was the smoke, thought Johnny.

With that the Knight of the Swan smiled. 'There is just one more thing,' he said. 'I am to take one of the Blessed with me.'

'Why?' said Johnny, more forcibly than he'd intended.

The knight smirked. 'Why do you think?' he said, going towards Anna and taking her by the hand.

Anna flinched. She did not want to go anywhere with the horrible man, but his grip was tight.

'You're hurting me,' she said, but the Knight of the Swan did not loosen his hold.

'I know that you are all very loyal people,' said the knight, 'and that you wouldn't dream of trying anything in my absence. With the king less well guarded, perhaps you might think it a good time to take some course of action. So, I am going to take you –' he kneeled down and stroked a strand of hair back from Anna's face – 'on a little journey to the port of Notus. It isn't far, my dearest, and there are lots of pretty sights along the way.' He stood up, carefully placing the locket that had come loose as he'd leaned down back beneath his undershirt.

Johnny realised what he was saying. 'You wouldn't,' he said.

'It is just a precaution,' said the knight gently.

'Let go of me!' said Anna, frightened.

'And if anything happens, if I hear from my informers that any of you have so much as planned to step out of this room, then this pretty little girl here . . . Well . . .'

'You wouldn't dare to hurt her,' said Selena.

'Who said anything about hurting?' said the knight. There was no doubt in anyone's mind what he meant. Anna started to wail and to beat at him with her fists. Smiling, he dragged Anna out of the room.

'The tower is crumbling,' Selena said softly, as the black wall closed after them. She walked to the window and rested her head on the glass. She didn't cry, but Johnny could tell that she was holding it in. He almost wanted to tell her to let it out, but felt it wouldn't be appropriate.

With a great deal of effort, she drew in her breath, turned, and faced Johnny. Johnny wanted to comfort her, but something in the majesty of her expression, in the glint of her eyes, prevented him. *She's still one of them*, thought Johnny. *Something . . . else.*

'They call you Blessed,' said Selena finally, after Johnny thought the silence might stretch and break into a million pieces. 'But, like me, you are the opposite. Cursed to die at the hands of my insane father. Look.' She gestured to the square below. 'They are preparing the scene of my Taking Apart already.' Black-clad servants were putting rows of seats up around the square, and raising a platform for the king to sit on.

'We'll find a way out of it,' Johnny said quietly.

And that was what made the princess cry. Not her approaching death, not the Knight of the Swan's frightening loyalty, not Anna being taken hostage, not her own father's madness, but the simple voice of a young man. She sat down on the ground in her long ceremonial gown and wept, and Johnny stroked her hair and whispered to her things that his own mother had said to comfort him when he was sad.

After a while, there was the sound of horns blowing from outside, and Selena wiped her eyes.

'What's your name?' said Johnny.

'I am the Silver Princess, daughter of the Ruler of the Silver Kingdom,' she said with some little pride.

'Your real name,' said Johnny. 'The thing that everyone calls you. So I'm John Frederick Williamson. But everyone calls me Johnny.'

The princess looked a little confused. Then she said, 'My name? My name . . . is Selena Candida of the Dark Tower . . . My mother . . . my mother called me Lena.'

'Then so will I,' said Johnny, and kissed her on the cheek. Selena's brow crinkled. *Maybe she's never been kissed before*, thought Johnny. 'What happened to her, Lena?' asked Johnny.

Selena fixed her expression. 'My mother . . . She was only his most recent queen. That's how he talks about it, when he remembers. "My most recent queen!" I have older half sisters, four of them, in a castle miles away, guarded night and day . . . But my mother . . . She was from the White Rocks of Zephyrus, the calm lake there, where the sun is gentle and the sweet trees blossom . . . I have only been there once. Her father – my grandfather – was the Knight of the White Rocks, and he kept the boundaries safe . . . His daughter was chosen as the king's wife. And I was her only child . . .'

'And where is she now? Is she with the Knight of the White Rocks?'

Selena leaned her forehead against the window. 'There is no Knight of the White Rocks now . . .' she whispered. 'Unless you count me. My mother was . . . Taken Apart with him. I was seven years old . . . The king made me watch it, and told me that she had betrayed him, and that I was going to live because he wanted me to learn that she was wrong . . . She blew me a kiss as she was tied to the horses. She didn't even cry . . .'

There was a moment of stillness.

Then came the sound of a soldier's roar from outside. Johnny went to the window and put his hands on Selena's shoulders.

'Look!' said Johnny quietly. 'They're leaving!'

Below them in the square was the Knight of the Swan, on a black horned horse that towered above the grooms holding it. He was in full black armour, and there was a man to his side holding a banner which fluttered in the wind. On it was the crescent moon that was the sign of the Kingdom, and beneath it was the Knight's swan. It was stylised, thin and silver, and it rippled so that it looked like it was alive.

'They're going on embassy,' said Selena softly.

The king himself was standing facing the knight and his attendants. He was saying something, and gesticulating wildly. Spit arced from his lips. Bruin stood ponderously on one side of him; Malek on the other. On a horned horse, seated in front of a soldier, was Anna – wrapped in a long white cloak, her face running with tears.

The king made a final gesture and horns sounded. The Knight of the Swan set off at a quick walk on his beautiful black horned horse, followed by perhaps a hundred soldiers. The king danced as they left.

Selena waited until the last soldiers had passed out of the square. Her old determination was back. She wouldn't let this setback stop her. Worse things had happened.

'I have something to tell you, Johnny,' she said. Outside the horns faded away, and clouds slid across the sun.

Johnny felt a peculiar lurch in his stomach. What was this strange, beautiful creature going to say?

Selena stretched out her arms. 'There is hope.

There is a way out. There is a way to topple the king.'

Johnny's guts were twisting.

'We can do it. We can do it together. And what's more, we have help. Help from elsewhere.'

A magehawk flew across the window, shadows flowing from its wings.

'Simon. Simon and Flora. They're here. Your siblings are here. Yours and Anna's.'

'Flora? Is she all right? How did she get here?' Johnny exclaimed. 'Does that mean we can get out? We can go home?'

Selena said with all the sureness of her rank, 'We will get out. Do not fear. And I will answer all your questions in time.' She sighed, and then all that could be heard was a soldier's trumpet blowing in the distance, announcing the passage of the Knight of the Swan.

Chapter Seventeen

THE PORT
OF NOTUS

I T WAS CHILLY inside the shade of the trees, and
Simon was huddled against a trunk. Flora was
banging her foot up and down on the grass. Pike was
swinging from a branch, when Eagret came running.
The Lady of the Stag, in conference with the rebels,
paused mid-sentence.

'The Knight of the Swan!' shouted Eagret.

Everyone jumped to their feet, scrambling to
grab their weapons.

'No, no, he's not coming here – he's going along
the road to the port of Notus. He's got many soldiers
with him. I was hiding behind a tree by the side of

the road – I overheard two of them talking. They're going on embassy to meet with the Realm.'

'So they'll execute the princess when they get back,' said Lavinia.

'They've . . . they've got one of the Blessed with them,' exclaimed the messenger.

'Which one?' said Simon apprehensively.

'The small girl.'

Anna! They had Anna! 'What are they doing to her? Is she all right?'

'She looks unhurt. They've got her on a horse, and they're riding slowly. They've got a large retinue, heavily armed, marching behind them. I imagine they've taken her as a hostage.'

'Why?' said Simon.

'I think they'll kill her if the princess tries anything,' said the messenger bluntly.

Kill her! 'I want to go,' said Simon suddenly. 'To the port of Notus.'

Everyone looked at him. He cleared his throat, embarrassed suddenly.

'I can't let anything happen to my sister. If anyone tries anything . . . I won't be able to sleep knowing she's there and in danger. I won't be any use to you. We can't do anything about the king whilst Anna's with them, anyway. And I want to see the embassy from the Golden Realm.'

'It's dangerous,' said Lavinia. 'I'm not sure that we can risk losing you.'

'I'll go with him,' said Flora.

Lavinia smiled at her courage. 'You are the only two people who can kill the king – I can't let you go without protection.'

'Then I'll go too,' said Pike, turning back to them. 'Simon's right. We can't do anything whilst Anna's a hostage – the knight will harm her if we try something on the king. I think we should go. It will be useful to us in gathering intelligence. We can follow them and keep an eye on Anna. It's only half a day's walk from here.'

Lavinia looked thoughtful. 'You could try to make contact with the Realm,' she said. 'But you will have to be extremely careful.'

'I don't want to make contact with them,' said Simon. 'I just want to see them.' But that wasn't quite true. He did want to make contact with them. He wanted to see them, and then he wanted to scream at them. He wanted to hurl his feelings at their infuriating, impassive faces, and demand why they had lied to him and to Flora.

'We don't have enough provisions,' said Lavinia. 'We're going to have to survive on what we can hunt from the forest, and berries and roots. There are deer here, and other creatures, and a stream flows near by.'

'I can hunt,' said Pike.

'I can learn,' said Flora.

They searched among their belongings. Somehow Simon had managed to hold on to his sack. In it were all the things from his rucksack. He sniffed. There was an apple in there, rotting slightly. He threw it to one side.

'You'd better take the hunting horn and the sunsword,' said Lavinia. 'But don't take anything . . . suspicious,' she continued, holding up Simon's sunglasses. 'What are these for?'

Simon indicated what to do, and she put them on. Simon allowed himself a momentary smile.

'Why on earth would you want to put things on your eyes that prevent you seeing well?' She took them off, puzzled, and handed them back to Simon. 'It's best if you go dressed as you are, like poor folk. Pike can sound like a countryman, and you two keep quiet. With three of you, less suspicion will be aroused. The countryside is freer than the city – there aren't so many soldiers around – but the port of Notus is a rough place.

Go there, find out what you can, and make sure that you leave before the embassy does. In the meantime, we will see if we can find a way to get into the city and the palace, without the princess. Whatever you do, don't make yourself known, and don't try to rescue Anna. Be careful,' finished Lavinia.

'We'll be back by the day after tomorrow at the latest,' said Pike. 'We'll spend a day there looking around and seeing what we can discover from the meeting.'

'And keeping an eye on Anna,' said Simon.

'And wondering about Johnny,' Flora added quietly.

'The embassy will be coming through a point of contact between the worlds, which is in the Hall of Sundering.'

'How are we going to get in there?' said Pike.

'You'll have to use your wits,' said Lavinia.

They took what they could. Scarlet had been foraging and shyly presented Pike with some roots and mushrooms. Simon hated the smell of them. 'You'll like them when you're hungry,' said Scarlet, and Pike winked at her. They had some berries as well, and took water from the nearby stream in flasks. They left everything else behind.

They travelled quickly, Pike leading them just

along the side of the road. It was a broad one, which, Pike explained, led due south to the port of Notus. Unimpeded by anything heavy, they soon caught up with the tail end of the Knight of the Swan's retinue – a couple of young, beefy soldiers – and Simon shivered at the sight of their glinting weapons. There were maybe a hundred soldiers in all, then the Knight of the Swan on his horse, and next to him, held in front of another soldier on a horse, was Anna, in a long white dress, doing her best to cause as much fuss as possible.

That sounds familiar, thought Simon, half-smiling to himself at her shouting.

'We musn't get too close to them,' said Pike, guiding them into the woods bordering the road.

Simon looked out through the trees, the black leaves disconcerting him. Anna was being handed a drink, of which she took a sip and then refused the rest. 'That's yukky,' she said. 'I want lemonade!'

The guard looked confused. 'What is lemonade?'

'You're all so stupid!' she replied. 'You don't know what chocolate is, or lemonade, or oranges, or anything normal. Only those stupid berries all the stupid time. And they don't even taste nice!'

The guard looked as if he was about to strike her, and it was all Simon could do not to rush out there and then. But the guard's fellow held his hand back. 'No touching,' he said. 'Orders of Sir Mark.'

The silver sun was quite high in the sky now, and the knight's retinue was moving onwards at a fairly swift pace, their weapons and armour clanking.

Simon started to feel better. All that time in the temple cave complex had dampened his spirits. He caught sight of Flora, who was looking intently ahead, and saw that her eyes were brighter, her cheeks tinged with colour. Pike seemed almost grown up, thought Simon, like a soldier himself. The black leaves whispered and rustled.

'What did your father not do?' said Simon. 'I mean, to get . . .'

Pike coughed. 'He refused to kill a woman,' he said. 'A serving lady in the palace. The king was testing his loyalty. He asked him to kill this woman – just picked her out of the crowd. And my father said no. For that, he was Taken Apart. And I will have my revenge.' He looked ahead. 'Now, we'll keep about a hundred paces behind them,' said Pike. 'They won't be expecting anyone to follow them. When we get there, we blend in with the townspeople, get as near to the Hall of Sundering as possible, and try to go in to hear what's happening. Then we can come straight back out, meet the others in the forest, and head back to the city. No waiting around, no surprises. Understood?'

Simon nodded, Flora smiled, and they slipped off through the trees, careful not to make any noise as they went.

Simon found that he wasn't really hungry. The roots in his sack were giving off a pungent smell, but, despite what Scarlet had said, he felt he didn't really want to eat them. His body seemed to have tightened in on itself, like a screw, and his energy to derive from some other source. *Maybe it's from you,* he thought, clutching at the black hunting horn. *What are you made from?*

Flora was having similar feelings about the sunsword. When she had it at her waist, she felt alive – more than alive. And on the rare occasions that she took it off, she felt everything else was duller. She wondered if that was how Johnny felt. Why he went back to his drugs, again and again. Was the world so flat to him? Could he find nothing so beautiful as what he saw in his mind? She felt the danger of it inside her.

The knight's procession paused one more time towards the middle of the afternoon, and Simon heard Anna crying out. He wanted to see what was happening, but Pike wouldn't let him, insisting instead he went quickly on his own. He returned a few minutes later, with a big grin on his face.

'What happened?' asked Simon anxiously.

'One of the guards was lifting Anna up on to her horse,' said Pike, 'and Anna bit him on his thumb.'

Good girl, thought Simon, relieved.

Soon they came to the edge of the forest. The road widened out into a broad plain covered in short, scrubby, dark grass, which curved gently down to the town and a bay beyond. The whitish expanse of the sea glistened, reaching out towards the horizon. The three of them paused in the shadows as the knight's party made its way to the town, banners fluttering.

The clear sea lapped against dark, stony shores. Smoke rose into the air from many chimneys. It was a settlement of a few hundred buildings. Unlike the king's city, though, these were all made from wood and stone. The sight of these houses, that could almost have been from back home, made Simon and Flora both gasp with delight.

'It'll be easy to get in,' said Pike, seeing that there appeared to be no gates, and few guards. 'No one will question us. The port isn't as busy as it used to be, but there are enough strange people around that nobody minds anyone else's business. It still trades

– boats go out from here up to the city of Zephyrus and then to the Borean Towers. And there,' he said, pointing to a large, stone, circular building that sat oppressively in the middle of the town, 'is the contact point between our world and the Golden Realm.'

'Is it like the standing stones between our worlds?' asked Flora.

The knight and his retinue were being met at the entrance to the town by a party of townspeople. The guards halted in formation, and Anna remained on her horse.

'Yes,' answered Pike. 'Except it's been blocked for ages. I imagine they're only going to open it a little way to let the embassy come through.'

Simon wondered if the same messengers who'd come to him back at his parents' cottage by the sea would be there. He remembered their impassive faces; their sense of warmth, of light, of . . . he could only call it goodness. Now the thought of them rolled around in his mind, confused, breaking apart.

A little while later, the townspeople stood by, and the Knight of the Swan rode into the port town, followed by his tramping guards. Simon heard Anna squealing.

'Is your sister always like that?' asked Flora.

Simon shrugged. 'Guess so.' But inwardly he smiled.

They waited a few more minutes, watching the sea wash against the beaches and a few boats gently sway on the waves with tall, thin sails of different colours – some red, some green, some black. Flocks of birds scattered in the air; a few lone walkers could be seen on the shoreline. Gulls swooped and perched, and a fish leaped out of the water and back again.

'Time to go in,' said Pike. 'If anyone asks, I'll say we're just down from a village a few miles in the north – Seven Stones – come to pick up some fish for our family. You two make sure you don't say anything.'

They set out towards the town. Houses were scattered on either side of the road, and Simon saw people going in and out of them, but nobody stopped to ask them anything or even to challenge them. *Too scared*, he thought, *even here.*

As the houses grew closer together, more and more people appeared on the road, all going to and fro. There was a tall, dark man with golden hair in a robe printed with flowers who smiled broadly at Simon and opened the robe to reveal a row of herbs dangling from the inside. 'Buy some sweetrest! Have some honeywort! Give you a chance with your lady!'

Simon blushed, and hoped that Flora hadn't noticed.

A little hound, dark and scraggy, was stalking around, sniffing at people's ankles. A woman, huge, swaying, carrying baskets of vegetables, sang as she walked. Their voices here were tinged with an accent a little different from the city people – softer round the edges. There were, of course, pictures of the king hanging from every available surface, be it trees, doors or windows. Simon even saw a man walking along holding a banner on which the king's white face fluttered unevenly in the sea breeze.

Sometimes a door to a house would open, and Simon would see into a corridor with a little child peeping out, but the doors would always slam shut.

Soon they were in the centre of the town. The Knight of the Swan's party had halted up ahead by a tall and graceful white house. It was clearly official, as the flag of the Kingdom swayed from a post attached to its upper storey. The guards thronged the small square, and around it the people of the port stood watching.

Pike whispered to Simon and Flora to wait, and they paused, looking at each other for the first time in ages. *She's changed*, thought Simon. *She's harder, somehow. And perhaps I am too.*

'Doesn't smell very salty, does it?' he said.

Flora smiled. 'I guess their sea probably isn't very much like ours.'

Simon nodded. It was very clear, for a start.

Flora said, 'It's so strange. A few days ago we didn't even know each other. I was Flora Williamson, living my life, and you were Simon Goldhawk, living yours. And now . . . all that we've seen together . . . Half of me still thinks it's a kind of dream, and I wish and wish that I could wake up and be in my bed again and hear Johnny playing some record, and Mum downstairs making breakfast. Bacon and eggs. *Crispy* bacon. And coffee! But it never does happen . . .'

'I never got to liking coffee,' said Simon. 'Tea for me.'

Flora took Simon's hand, and Simon felt a surge of affection for her. He was about to mumble something when Pike came back.

'They're staying in there,' he said, pointing at the graceful building. 'Well, the Knight of the Swan is. The guards are in the barracks opposite. And I heard the knight say that they were meeting the embassy tomorrow morning. So we'd better find somewhere to stay tonight.'

And then tomorrow, thought Simon, *tomorrow we will see the messengers of the Golden Realm.*

Chapter Eighteen

SPEAKING
SNAKE

THE OWNER OF the lodging house was thin and absent-looking, and clearly used to many people coming and going. She barely glanced at the three friends as they asked if she had a room, and simply stood aside to let them into the narrow corridor. The walls were damp and there was a dank, rotting smell.

'The Ritz this is not,' whispered Flora to Simon as they went in.

'A quarter crescent each,' the woman shouted at them as they went past and clambered up the creaky stairs. 'And you provide your own food.'

It was a small, dark, damp room, and there was

only one bed, so Pike and Simon made do down on the floor, whilst Flora self-consciously took the narrow mattress and lay there, shivering a little as the wind whistled through cracks in the walls, sleeping on and off until morning and thinking of her soft bed at home. Simon didn't sleep well either.

Pike's dreams were haunted by the cold features of the Knight of the Swan.

How long has it been, thought Pike, *since my father was killed? Killed – murdered, executed, Taken Apart.* Before he fell asleep, Pike found himself going over what had happened, and before he knew it, he was deep inside his memories, as if he were reliving them.

The Knight of the Shark came into the dining hall, where Pike was sitting by the fire. He flung down his spear, his face was white and tight like Pike had never seen it before . . . He sent all the servants away, and drained a beaker of wine, then another, and then he dashed it to the floor. It broke, and the wine spilled, and Pike couldn't help but think it looked like blood.

Then he tried to tell me something, Pike remembered.

'The Knight of the Swan,' Pike's father had said. 'The king – he's insane. They're doing things to the world I cannot even understand . . .' And then the doors had burst open – the king's guards with the royal hounds, and Sir Mark, the Knight of the Swan, had come rushing in. They'd taken him, and Pike's father hadn't said anything more.

Knowing what usually happened to the families of those Taken Apart, Pike had lost no time in escaping from the family tower. Disguised, he'd watched his father's execution from the crowd, and his heart ached to think that his father had died believing that nobody he loved had come to see it.

And then he'd run through the city until he didn't know where he was, and he'd scrabbled around the backstreets and listened to rumours and followed trails until he'd found the Lady of the Stag. They'd taken him in and fed and clothed him and primed him for revenge. He felt that word as if it were cut deeply into his bones.

Revenge.

And he was ready for it.

Early the next morning, they were standing in the shade under the eaves of a house not quite opposite the Hall of Sundering. It loomed above them, a circular building made out of grey stone, at whose door stood two well-armed guards. There seemed to be no windows, only tiny little slits right at the top of the wall.

People were trundling carts and barrows, but none were full; they had only small loads of fish, spices and cloths, and many of the people were also simply standing about. News of the embassy had travelled far, and the town's population was curious; they were fascinated, too, by the Knight of the Swan, whose name struck terror into so many hearts. The people here were dressed more brightly than in the king's city. Simon saw reds and greens, and even a flash of gold at someone's ear. A parrot-like bird, crimson and blue, fluttered from the roof above them, and swooped down on to a barrow, flying off with a fish in its mouth. The trader shook his fist after it and swore.

'How on earth are we going to get in?' whispered Flora to Pike.

'Hmmm . . .' said Pike. 'Let's go round the back.' And, first checking that they were not observed by person or by magehawk, he ducked into the alley behind them. Picking over piles of rubbish, he led them through a series of narrow, unpaved streets up round the back of the hall.

'The king built this when the realms were sundered,' Pike said as they stood, gazing up at the hall's bulk. 'This used to be the main point of contact between us and the Realm. There's no back door . . .'

It looked terribly forbidding: a dark mass, with no hint of a break in its walls.

Flora looked doubtfully at the sunsword. 'Do you think it could cut a way in?'

'I don't know,' said Pike. 'Try it on this stone.'

With a look of concentration on her face, Flora unsheathed the sunsword. Its warmth and brilliance were welcoming to Simon. She aimed at a large stone that lay on the ground, and brought the shining blade down on to it.

The stone went bright orange, hissed, crumbled and vanished.

Flora resheathed the sunsword. 'Effective, but I guess we don't want to destroy the whole building,' she said, a little shakily.

Simon wondered if maybe the horn could have a helpful effect. What was it Flora had said? *The walls came tumbling down . . . The walls of Jericho.* He could adjust the tone of the horn so that it had a smaller or larger effect on things, the Lady of the Stag had said. He pulled it off his shoulder and inspected it carefully, its strange black mass cold.

'Do you think,' he said, 'that if I blew this – very gently – it might make an opening, a crack in the wall that we could go through? Lavinia said it was a weapon, after all, didn't she?'

'Let's experiment first,' said Flora.

Pike nodded. 'I think that's wise. It's a very special horn – ancient and powerful. And I don't even know how powerful.' Pike looked around the quiet street, and saw another pair of rocks resting against a wall. He pointed them out to Simon.

'You see those? Try to focus on them. Try to split one so that it doesn't break in two, but just cuts a way through.'

Simon took a deep breath, expelled it, then drew in a shallower one, and put the hunting horn to his lips. Immediately its weird power flooded through him, and the flash and rip of reality that had happened when he'd first blown it came vividly back to him. He saw too the carter, hurled backwards and into unconsciousness by its force.

Not that much power, thought Simon. *Not that hard.* He pictured the stones in his mind, imagined them filling with sound and then gently splitting, just halfway to the top, creating a space that went all the way through.

Without looking at either Flora or Pike, he poured all his concentration in to the stones, and then blew a low, gentle note that sank into the air and died.

Simon slowly put the horn down, watching the stones. Nothing happened.

'Never mind,' said Flora. 'We'll find another way . . .'

There was a crack, and the larger of the stones split gently from its base up to about halfway. Simon ran over to it and picked it up. 'Hey!' he said. 'Look!' He poked a stick through it.

Good, he thought. *Now for the building.*

'What do you know about the inside of the hall?'

'There's a long corridor going all the way around the central hall, and in the centre is the contact point,' Pike told them.

'How on earth are we going to do this without anyone noticing?' said Simon. 'You said it was guarded inside, right?'

Pike raised his eyebrows. 'Yes . . .'

Simon was hesitating when Flora said, 'Look! What's that?'

It was a flash of gold – a gold that she recognised from the messengers. Surely they hadn't already arrived? And if they had, what were they doing creeping about on the ground?

Coming quickly towards them was a little golden serpent. Pike put his hands over his mouth, and dropped to his knees.

'What is he doing?' whispered Flora to Simon. The snake approached Pike and, to Simon and Flora's amazement, coiled itself slowly around his arm.

'Pike!' hissed Flora.

Pike looked back, beaming. 'It's all right,' he said. And then he kissed the snake's head. Something happened to Simon's vision, then. He was seeing Pike and the snake, but at the same time, overlaying the snake was another image, flickering in and out of sight, and larger than it – a woman, tall and graceful, her hand on Pike's arm. And Pike was looking up at her with love and devotion, tears shining in his eyes.

The snake now seemed to be having some kind of conversation with Pike, who was nodding his head and looking first very pleased, then very thoughtful. After a little while the snake uncoiled itself, and Pike stood up, wiping his eyes.

'What's the matter?' said Simon.

'I'll tell you in a minute. Hurry,' Pike said. 'She says she can show us a way in.' The little golden creature slithered off round the side of the building.

'Oh really?' said Simon. 'And how can you tell that?'

Pike looked surprised. 'Because she told me.'

'What? Speak Parseltongue, do you?' said Flora.

'I don't know what that means,' said Pike.

'Oh,' said Flora. 'Of course you don't. It's in a book about a boy wizard . . . At home. I liked it when I was younger.'

'I don't know about that,' said Pike, looking confused, 'but of course I know what the snake's saying. Not that she's really a snake. That's just the shape she's in.'

They followed the snake round the wall until they came to a place where it stopped and pointed with her golden, arrow-shaped head, hissing quietly. There was a small chute leading out of the wall – small, but large enough to climb through.

'That's a . . . waste pipe,' said Pike.

'From the kitchens?' asked Flora.

'Yes. They won't have been used for ages. She says not to risk the horn, to keep quiet, and to get back to Lavinia as soon as possible.'

'Who says?' said Simon and Flora at the same time.

'Why, my mother, of course,' said Pike, as he held both sides of the pipe and looked in, then put a hand to his nose. 'The Lady of the Snake. Coming?'

And as he disappeared into the chute, the golden snake vanished, leaving Simon and Flora staring at each other, totally dumbfounded.

'After you,' said Flora.

Simon took a deep breath and followed Pike.

Chapter Nineteen

THE EMBASSY
FROM THE REALM

I T WASN'T SO bad in the chute. There was only a faint smell of mustiness and rotten food, and Simon soon found himself tumbling out after Pike into a small room illuminated by the dim light from one of the slits in the wall above them. It was a kitchen, dusty and unused.

'So that was your mother?' said Flora, exiting the chute and brushing herself down.

'Yes,' said Pike. 'The Lady of the Snake. She was from the Golden Realm, and she was exiled from this world long before my father was . . . killed.

She was helping the princess . . .'

'How did she get into the Kingdom?' asked Simon.

'The Way must already have been opened for the embassy from the Golden Realm,' said Pike. 'Now follow me, and don't make a sound.'

He went briskly to the door. Simon was glad he hadn't had to use the hunting horn. He didn't know if he could control it properly yet, and it might have attracted too much attention.

Flora, on the other hand, was upset about not being able to deploy the sunsword. It had been a while since she had used it properly and felt its golden, warm power. She felt that the world needed that power. It was so dank and dark and gloomy. The room around her seemed to be closing in, the darkness to shiver. She was always afraid of the shadows now.

Pike opened the door slightly, and then immediately closed it again.

'Guards?' said Simon.

Pike nodded. He peered out again. There was a narrow corridor that curved round the inside of the whole building. It was almost completely dark.

'Patrolling,' said Pike. He pressed his eye to the crack of the door and waited. Simon couldn't tell how long it was before Pike turned to them again.

'Two guards with lit torches. They're coming round regularly. We'll wait till they're halfway, round the other side, and then make a dash for the central hall. Ready?'

In the silence Simon tried to keep his breathing quiet. He wondered if he should feel for Flora's hand. What was she thinking about? Not for the first time he thought about what it would be like to see her back at home.

Then Pike opened the door, and it was time to go. Pike paced slowly, keeping close to the wall. Simon followed next, and checked behind to make sure Flora was there. She touched his fingertips.

They crept round the edges, until Pike suddenly held up his hand. There was a murmur of voices from ahead. Pike peered round. He could see quite well. There was a glimmer of torchlight here, and people moving towards a large double doorway. He saw the pale face of the Knight of the Swan, and drew back instinctively, his heart beating fast.

When the last of the knight's people had gone through the door, Pike forced himself to count slowly to fifty. The patrolling guards would be upon them soon, but they couldn't risk going in so quickly after the knight.

Simon was biting his lip, Flora standing rigid. Then Pike pressed forwards, and gently pushed open the door to the main chamber and peered through the crack.

Ahead in the grand central circle was the embassy from the Broken King, consisting of the Knight of the Swan, ten soldiers, and Anna, who was sitting on her own looking sulky, the golden coronet askew on her head. The soldiers held torches, which cast a dim glow.

In the centre of the circle was a standing stone. And around it, bathed in radiance, was the embassy from the Golden Realm.

Gently, Pike edged further in, and the three of them slipped into the shadows and crouched by the door, which softly clicked shut.

Simon had to hold in a gasp. There was his original messenger, and Flora's, no longer astride a bird-deer, but standing tall, and they were no longer entirely golden: their faces were not gold and impassive, but human and alive. Behind them was a tall, grave, young man whom Pike, with a leap of joy in his heart, recognised as Mithras.

And there was Raven, her long black hair now neatly coiled, her serious expression so different from the laughing, singing girl they'd known in London. There, too, was the Lady of the Snake, Pike's mother in her true form as a woman with a golden necklace in the shape of a snake. Beside her was Hover. The flying man.

Behind them was a gash in the air, through which Simon caught glimpses of golden things moving. *Is that their world?* he thought. An idea occurred to him. *Can I just grab Anna and run through into the Golden Realm?* It would be exciting to explore another world, a golden world where Hover came from . . . But would they be safe there?

They used us, he reminded himself. *They threw us into danger* But despite himself he felt their power, their warmth, and he remembered the gentle, energy-giving touch of the bird-deer's muzzle as he sat by the stream back at home.

The Knight of the Swan was speaking. 'We welcome the embassy from the Golden Realm,' he said in courtly tones.

Mithras answered him, bowing slightly, and holding his hands together as if in prayer. 'The Silver Kingdom has committed an act of war.'

'The Golden Realm oversteps the mark, as usual,' said the Knight of the Swan, scoffing. 'We have opened the Way for you, but we have heard rumours that you have been seen in other places.'

'That is beside the point,' said Mithras calmly. 'The Silver Kingdom has attacked a servant of our queen Helena, when you struck our emissary Hover. If you refer to the treaty made at the time of the Sundering, that constitutes an act of war. You must accept our terms,' said Mithras, 'or we will attack.'

'Go on,' said the knight.

'The Kingdom must comply. If it does not, then we will be on a war footing.'

'Your terms, Mithras,' said the knight, managing to show elegant contempt in a curl of his lip.

'One: you must depose King Selenus, known to us as the Broken King.'

'Never!' shouted the knight.

'Two: you must place on the throne in his stead the Silver Princess, Selena.'

The knight smiled wryly.

'Three: you must release the prisoners from the other world, that you call Blessed, and return them safely with their siblings to their own lands.'

At least they've remembered us now, thought Simon.

The Knight of the Swan laughed, and then started to clap his mailed hands together, the sound ringing in the echoing chamber. 'And what makes you think that we will comply with your ridiculous demands?'

'You do not want war, do you, Sir Mark? You have said so yourself.'

Pike, Simon and Flora huddled together, watching keenly.

The Knight of the Swan drew himself up.

'My Lord Mithras,' he said, 'you have played us well. You have sent your messenger to us through those children. You have put us in an interesting position. I am the ambassador of my king. I am his voice, his arm, his law. I tell you now . . .' His voice grew louder. '. . . that the Silver Kingdom will not give way to the Golden Realm! And it is meet that I inform you that your treacherous pawn, the Silver Princess, is in fetters, and will be Taken Apart the day after tomorrow!'

There were gasps from the Golden Realm's group. Mithras bent urgently to the Lady of the Snake and whispered something; the others put their heads together.

'Yes, yes,' said the Knight of the Swan. 'I know all about it. I know how the Silver Princess – though she is no longer worthy of that name – has been the woodworm in the palace, eating away at our foundations! I know that you, my Lady of the Snake, have used your own son Pike to lead your emissary here! Your plans are all revealed to us. And know this: we will not stand for them! We give you these conditions.'

Mithras stepped forwards. 'Be careful, Knight of the Swan.'

'You dare to warn me?' said the knight, in a low voice that somehow Simon found far more frightening.

'You do not know with what you are dealing,' said Mithras, his voice ringing gentle and clear.

'These are our conditions,' said the knight, suddenly drawing his sword. Neither Mithras nor any of the embassy from the Golden Realm flinched. 'Leave this Kingdom. Close the Way. Do not enter here – nor you nor any other from your Realm. You will leave the Blessed Ones to us, and their siblings too.'

'And if we do not agree?' said Mithras quietly.

The knight flung down his sword. 'Then prepare yourselves.'

'We wait on the borders, knight. We have ways of getting in to your kingdom. There are other ways, older ways, and we are finding ever more. You are not the only one with secret knowledge. We have felt you and your king, rooting around in the darker places . . . You cannot shut us out for ever,' said Mithras. He bowed to the knight, and made a sweeping gesture. A ball of light appeared between his hands; it grew and grew and then burst in a flash. Everyone in the hall had to put their hands over their eyes. In the confusion, the Golden embassy stepped through the gash.

The Knight of the Swan cried out in annoyance. The light vanished and the room was dark as night, the gash closed.

When their eyes readjusted, the Knight of the Swan stood there staring, then swung round suddenly. Pike, Simon and Flora shrank back into the shadows as he marched out, followed by his soldiers, taking Anna with them. Once more, she passed so close to Simon that if he had dared to, he could have reached out and touched her.

They sat in the darkness, trying to hold on to the warmth of the Golden people, going over in their minds what they had seen and heard. Just before they decided to go, Simon heard something moving. Turning, he saw a flash of gold. There was nothing there, but he wondered if perhaps one of them had stayed behind.

They went out through the chute. Outside in the silver light Simon noticed that the others were worn and tired. The Hall of Sundering rose up above them, grey and fearsome, and he was glad to have got out of it.

Through the bustling streets they returned to their lodgings, paid the thin lady and gathered their belongings. Whilst Pike went to find out where the Knight of the Swan was and what he was doing, the other two set out for the road to their camp in the forest.

Leaving the town, they turned to watch the sea and feel the sun on their faces. Simon smiled at Flora. 'I'm sure Johnny's all right,' he said. 'Anna looked like she was healthy, at least.'

'I'm sure he is,' said Flora. 'I just want to see him up close . . .' Before she knew it, tears sharpened in her eyes. She gripped the handle of the sunsword and let its strength rush through her, wondering when she would get to use it properly. And why she wanted to so much.

The battering of hooves on the road warned them of someone approaching, and they made themselves inconspicuous in the woods. A moment later, Pike appeared, riding a horned horse and leading another.

'Get on, quickly,' he said, when they stepped out. 'You two share. We'll make our way back. We've got to hurry. The knight leaves tonight.'

Simon put out his hand to help Flora, but she jumped on, using the stirrup confidently and settling into the rudimentary saddle. She held the reins with a practised air. 'This guy looks like he can go quite fast,' she said. 'Coming?'

'Where did you get these horses?' said Simon.

'I . . . borrowed them,' replied Pike. 'I won't forget where from.'

Riding steadily, they made the journey back to the cave in the forest before the sun reached halfway across the sky.

Pike told them about the Knight of the Swan. The Taking Apart would be a day earlier.

'We leave now,' said Lavinia, nodding curtly, barely giving them time to dismount. 'We'll have to improvise. We rescue the princess, and as for your siblings . . . We'll see.'

The trees rustled as people gathered their things, and Simon prepared himself for the final push. *Almost there now*, he thought, and took a draught of the hot, spicy drink they made.

Soon, silently, they set off towards the city, to rescue a princess, and to kill a king.

Chapter Twenty

Taken
Apart

SELENA GASPED AND struggled out of a dream. Something was clamping her down, something shapeless and nameless. With a great effort of will, she broke through and pulled herself into the waking world. Then, as she opened her eyes wider, she saw the Knight of the Swan standing in front of her, in his close-fitting black armour, a helm on his head with silver swan's wings on either side. There were four soldiers behind him.

'We came back early,' said the knight. 'Those friends of yours gave me reason to wish to expedite this matter. Bring the other one,' he commanded.

The soldiers marched forwards, and attached chains to Johnny.

'Coward!' shouted Johnny at the knight.

Sir Mark, sneering, strode forwards and slapped Johnny across the face. The blow was hard, and Johnny all but fell.

'If you knew what I have done in the service of my king, you would not call me coward,' said Sir Mark in a low tone.

The guards came to Selena with chains, but she shook her head, and said, 'If you think that I will not face my death calmly, then you do not know me at all.'

'I would say that was truly worthy of the daughter of a king,' said the knight, 'if you were not so debased.'

'Your loyalty, Knight of the Swan,' said Selena, 'will see you doomed.'

'Better to be doomed for my loyalty,' snarled the knight, 'than for treachery!'

'It is my father who is the traitor,' replied Selena. 'He has betrayed our kingdom. Who is to say that he will not turn against you as well?'

If a flicker of worry crossed over the knight's face, nobody noticed; the Knight of the Swan simply nodded curtly and said, 'Very well. Follow me. You guards, bring the boy.'

They straggled along a dark corridor, Johnny's chains clinking as they went, then came through a large set of doors which were opened for them. Johnny was paying very careful attention. He did not recognise where they were going, and was noting every window, every door.

They were joined by a small troop of soldiers leading royal hounds; the beasts were drooling and pulling on their leashes. Johnny stumbled and fell, and one of the hounds pounced at him. It was a horrible thing that seemed to have fur and scales and its mouth was in a strange place. Its eyes were red, and it stank of sweat and musk and worse things. Snarling, it dribbled over Johnny before a guard beat it off him.

They went along more dark corridors, and then into a huge glass hall. Below was a crowd of courtiers, knights and ladies, some in armour, some in brightly coloured clothing decorated with extraordinary, stylised animals. Banners stood unfurled, carried by servants – lions and bears and dragons and other beasts, all shimmering. There was Andaria, the green rider, filing her nails with a knife; there was Bruin the giant with his arms folded, and Malek the dwarf looking expectantly at the top of the stairs. Everyone was silent.

The Knight of the Swan halted and, smiling, declared, 'Behold! I bring you the traitor! The renegade princess herself!'

And then something terrible happened. The assembled crowd, eyes staring, expressionless, neutral, began to clap. In time, together, slowly, as the Knight of the Swan went down the stairs, and as the Princess Selena of the Silver Kingdom, daughter of Selenus, followed.

When they came to the bottom, the courtiers stopped clapping and made a passage for them. The little group, led by the growling and sniffing hounds, passed through. A lady in bright purple decorated with butterflies quietly clenched her fists; a young knight, his helmet crowned with peacock feathers, blinked, his forehead briefly creasing.

Johnny looked around, wondering why no one said anything, why no one rose up?

But he knew the answer: because one of them would be next. It would be one of them who stood on the platform. One of them Taken Apart.

Light streamed through the glass ceiling and illuminated the grand double doors at the end of the hall, and these opened to let them out.

Outside was a raised platform, on which the

king was enthroned in a scarlet and gold palanquin. His horns gleamed, the shadowy fuzz around him crackled. He laughed and clapped his hands. Anna was already there, her chin on her hand, chained to his throne.

All around the square were tiers of seats, all full. People were crowding in everywhere, even hanging off the statue of Silvanus. Magehawks perched in rows on railings, chattering and vanishing as if off reporting elsewhere.

It was the people's silence that was unbearable, far more than the watching eyes. Bruin the giant appeared and led Johnny to where Anna was. She greeted him silently. She had obviously been crying and looked exhausted.

The courtiers all filed out from the palace, and took their places on the platforms on either side of the king: a great, many-coloured, silent, and beautiful throng.

In the square were four horned horses, and attached to the neck of each horse was a thick rope, the other ends of which trailed to the ground.

The king stood up and held out his arms, addressing the crowd. 'My people! Know this! That any traitor will be Taken Apart. Any! Even my very daughter.'

There was no sadness in his voice. Indeed, he seemed to be almost exultant.

Nobody in the square or on the tiers of seats moved at the king's words.

The trees were fringed with the rolled-up structures that were the remains of those Taken Apart. Selena heard them clicking against each other, and into her mind came the image of a giant man grinding his teeth.

'Sir Mark! My dear knight – do you please lead the renegade to the horses.'

One of them, as if it knew what was going to happen, whinnied. The royal hounds started barking; their guards made no attempt to quieten them.

This is the moment of my death, thought Selena. *These past few years, since I was a mere girl of twelve, I've plotted and dreamed. And now it will all fail. My kingdom, my father, will come to nothing, and nothing can come from nothing*

The horned horses were pawing at the ground and snorting.

Sir Mark took Selena by the shoulder, but she shook off his hand and walked calmly to the edge of the platform from where a short flight of steps led to the square and the waiting beasts. Men wearing black and silver hoods stood, holding the heads of the horses. Selena was discomfited by the hoods. She found herself scanning the crowd for Clara, for her hound, but could not see them.

The king paced up and down before his palanquin, up and down, whilst his dwarf Malek and his giant Bruin stood implacably behind him. Behind them stood Andaria, her chin raised, her expression fathomless, and next to her the two Blessed Ones – Johnny testing his chains, Anna keeping still. The little monkey creatures skittered and chattered beside them.

The king came to a sudden stop before Selena, and took a slow step towards her. He inspected her. Then he said, surprising as a lightning bolt from a clear sky, 'Repent.'

A murmur arose from the courtiers. A shout came from the crowd.

The king came nearer to his daughter. He clasped her right shoulder, sending shockwaves of fear through Selena's body. His robes were embroidered with silver horns, and his face, up close, looked stretched. His eyes were wild and black as a beast's. He gazed at her as if completely detached. There was nothing human there, nothing that Selena could recognise or hold on to.

Father ... thought Selena. *He is my father.* Something deep inside her trembled and fluttered and almost broke.

'Repent!' whispered the king, grinning. 'Repent, and I will free you and forgive you. You will rule by my side, and we will fight the Golden Realm together – and conquer!'

I could, thought Selena. *I could do that. I could step away, renounce my rebellion, join him.* She imagined herself, enthroned and bejewelled, standing by him at his throne. She would have such power, such beauty in her power; she imagined all the knights kneeling to her, the feathers of their crests bobbing as they bent their helmeted heads. *I could rule them all,* she thought.

But then the picture in her mind changed, and she saw herself presiding over executions, saw the shuffling masses of the poor and the hungry. Saw the crowd, all gazing at her, intent.

They need me, she thought, turning her mind back to the present. *They need me to be a martyr. There are still rebels out there. And Simon and Flora, too,* she thought. *The ones who can still bring him down.*

She glanced over the crowd. Was that the Lady of the Stag, deep in their midst? She couldn't quite tell.

No, she thought. *I will face up to what I did. I will die, and I will be a martyr to the cause. Many will follow where I lead, and he will be overthrown in the end.*

She took a step back away from her father, lifting his hand gently off her shoulder.

'My dearest, darling,' he said. But there was still nothing in his voice that Selena could recognise as the father she had once known.

'I am not your darling,' she whispered. She took a deep breath, and raised her voice, facing out to the square. The wind blew back her hair; behind her the palace shone. The banners of the knights shook and shivered. She noticed, madly, a dragon on one of the banners, something she'd loved as a child. It gave her strength.

'They call me renegade,' she shouted. 'I am no such thing.'

This time the courtiers' muttering was so loud that the Knight of the Swan had to silence them with a shout.

'You live under a shadow. I, Selena Candida of the Dark Tower, princess of the Silver Kingdom; I am your true leader.'

Was that a call of approval from the crowd? They shifted, rolled, hooted. The little monkey creatures hissed and spat and threw nuts at her.

The king clicked his teeth.

'Kill me, and others will spring up in my place. I renounce you,' she said, turning to the king, her heart breaking. 'I renounce you and your deeds. I accept this, my martyrdom, with gladness. My people!' she said, and again, somebody in the distance shouted in support.

And then she realised. In the hall, when she was shown to the courtiers, they had been applauding her. The thought swirled through her. *They will succeed,* she thought. *They will.*

'Take her, take her,' said the king, hitching his robes up. He sighed deeply and waved at Bruin and Malek, who hesitated. 'Go on!' He clicked his fingers. 'So be it.'

Bruin and Malek came forwards and took her by the arms, and pulled her, not ungently, down the steps to where the horned horses stood in readiness.

They seemed so large, their shoulders so broad, their hooves so massive that Selena suddenly became very frightened indeed.

But she did not struggle.

Johnny clanked his chains. 'Do something!' he shouted to the crowd.

Nobody paid any attention to him.

Bruin and Malek led Selena to the centre of the square made by the horses, and lifted her on to her back, placing her on to the ground, then took up a rope each, tying them to her wrists.

I mustn't scream, Selena thought. *I mustn't.*

The courtiers rustled their skirts and their swords. Bruin and Malek were tying knots tightly around her ankles. They retreated, and she saw in their faces a deep compassion. *They are people*, she thought, *like me. They are just doing what they are told. But can I forgive them?*

Then she heard a voice. The Knight of the Swan. 'Two paces forward.'

The horses, goaded by the men in black and silver hoods, lifted their powerful shoulders, and pulled. Selena was stretched and lifted off the ground. She hung suspended, the ropes biting into her skin, making it burn unpleasantly.

'Comfortable?' said the knight. 'Now. Two more.'

The ropes strained again, the horses moved forwards, and that was when Selena started to feel the burning pain in her joints. She gritted her teeth.

'One more.'

Why is he doing this? thought Selena. Her vision

was starting to blur. *Why doesn't he just get it over with?*

The pain was now filling her body and, unable to bear it any longer, she screamed. It came from the bottom of her bowels and rang out over the square. A young squire fainted, and was carried quickly away by his relatives.

Selena's mind was growing fuzzy, filling with images from her childhood. *Concentrate on them, and do not feel the pain.* Her father – no, not him. Her mother – a flash of sweetness, of the sharp berries from the bushes in the Stone Gardens, and huge, bright flowers in her mother's arms as she laid them down on a table, ready to put in a red and gold painted vase.

Selena felt her shoulder dislocate, popping out of its joint. Heard words coming from far off, but could not understand them.

Everything was light, the pain had transformed into light, and she was becoming it too, turning into nothing but silver rays. *I will go back into the world,* she thought, *back through the light, back into nothing, back to the beginning and the end, and the goddesses who sang, and the snake will eat me and I will become nothing.*

Her thoughts coiled up into a knot of pain, and she fainted.

The Knight of the Swan was about to give his final order, the one for the horses to run, the one that would see the Silver Princess torn apart, limb from limb. There was a menacing air to the crowd: most of the townspeople's faces were carefully blank; others were obviously disgusted, and he saw fear in their eyes.

The knight knew she had rebelled against her king, and must pay the consequences. It was an honour for him to perform this execution. And it would show them all.

'Prepare yourselves for the final charge,' he cried.

The crowd wavered. The horses snorted. The king stared ahead, tapping his fingers on the arms of his throne. The Blessed Ones sat frozen in horror.

'At the count of three,' called the Knight of the Swan, 'let the horses run!'

The courtiers stood up as one. The crowd surged, people were crushed in the square.

'Three,' yelled the knight.

The princess was unconscious, suspended.

'Two.' The knight drew his sword and held it in the air, the sun shining off it. He flashed it downwards and shouted, 'One!'

The horses began to run, the ropes strained,

the crowd roared, and Selena was startled awake. Everything was fiery and this was the end, it was her death and it was burning her up and she cried out into the terrible darkness.

A thud. And then another heavier thud. What was this? The pressure on her legs was gone. It felt like they were going to float up into the air. Now the two horses dragging her arms were confused and stamping their hooves, and now they were trying to pull her forwards, but they couldn't because she was tied to something heavy, and they were neighing and whinnying, and they were dragging her, and yes, she still would die, it was going to happen . . . Then somebody cut the ropes binding her feet, and they fell to the ground as she felt her arms also go free.

Somebody lifted her up, put her on to a horse, and sat behind her.

She looked round blearily. She recognised him. It was . . . How could it be? It was the boy from the other world. Simon.

And there was Flora, leaping up on to the other horned horse.

'Don't move!' shouted someone, and there was the Lady of the Stag, standing on the statue in the middle of the square, holding a bow, an arrow notched into it, a quiver on her back. 'I have an arrow trained on you. We have archers all round the square.'

'My soldiers will cut you down,' said the knight calmly.

Guards were already making their way towards the statue, the townspeople ducking away from them.

'Simon!' It was Anna. She'd seen him. 'Simon! Help me!'

And Johnny was standing too, and waving as much as his chains would allow.

'Flora!'

The king gripped the arms of his throne and crossed his legs. 'My Lady of the Stag,' he said. 'I remember you. You are the sister of the Knight of the Shark. He had been my favourite.'

'When you were sane,' said the lady, 'my king.'

The king flared his nostrils and fondled his horns gently.

The soldiers marched onwards, and Lavinia loosed an arrow. It stuck, quivering, in a fold of the king's robe. She notched another, fast as sound.

'You were always the finest shot in the court,' said the king. 'But you know that no arrow can penetrate my shadow.'

'That is true,' said Lavinia. 'But there are others

who can be hurt.' And she shot the Knight of the Swan.

The arrow struck him in the eye, and he fell to his knees with a terrible, animal groan.

That was the signal. Flora and Simon, with the princess in front of him, urged on their horses and galloped through the square as the crowd fled. Arrows flew at the king's soldiers from the edges, where Eagret and Scarlet and the others were concealed.

Flora came to the statue. She reined in her horse, and held it still. The Lady of the Stag shot once more and then leaped on to the back, immediately turning around and shooting at the running guards.

Simon and Selena were racing towards the far end of the square. Royal hounds tore after them. One was felled by an arrow, but another leaped at Simon's horned horse and bit into its flank.

The horned horse, exhausted and terrified, had had enough; it reared and shook Selena off. Simon fell after her, and the horse bolted.

'To the princess!' called the Lady of the Stag, coming off Flora's horse.

A cart was lumbering towards them from the other side of the square, drawn by two horned horses, and with a robed figure at the reins. It was Pike.

The royal hounds were circling Selena and Simon, jaws slavering and piggy red eyes staring, fur bristling and scales shining. One leaped at Simon and bit him on the leg. Flora set her jaw and rode straight at them. They scattered, barking, but regrouped to the side, snarling.

The soldiers reached the centre, and trapped them in a square of bristling lances and swords. Flora backed her horse up to protect Simon and Selena.

Pike came trundling forwards with the cart. The arrows had stopped; Scarlet, Eagret and the others had fallen back to their hiding places as the guards advanced. Lavinia checked her quiver. Only two arrows left. Simon was hurt; Selena could hardly move. Simon managed to help her up to her feet, and saw the cart.

The king himself was approaching, through the now all but empty square. The courtiers had left the tiered seating and were now thronging their balconies, watching from the safety of their towers; the townspeople were crowding at the edges.

'Kill them,' said the king, without preliminary.

'Simon!' Anna's voice came from the throne, carried on the breeze.

Simon's heart, despite himself, filled with gladness.

'Don't worry, Anna!' he called back.

The soldiers advanced. The Lady of the Stag shot at them, bringing one of them down. One arrow left. The royal hounds got ready to pounce.

Five of them were circling Simon. Their tongues were out. They gave off a terrible stink.

Flora rushed her horse at the guards, gripping on to the bridle, unsheathing the sunsword and its radiance bathed the square. Immediately the guards fell back. She slashed at one, who tripped away; the others sprang away, uncertain, their faces lit in the fiery light.

'What are you waiting for?' came a voice. It was the Knight of the Swan. His right eye was a ragged mess. 'He's just a boy. Attack him!'

A royal hound rushed at Flora's horse and bit into its leg. Screaming, the horse bolted. The king was laughing as Flora's horse, out of control, galloped along the side of the square. Desperately she reined it in and managed to get it under control.

'Stay back!' she called. 'This is the legendary sunsword, torn from its hiding place where Mithras was imprisoned! Stay back and let us pass!'

'Flora!' Simon shouted. A royal hound was grabbing his injured leg with its teeth, and grizzling over him. He shook his leg but the hound's grip was tight.

Flora raced back over and slashed the sunsword at the guards, and they edged backwards. Pike jumped off the cart and ran quickly to Simon and Selena, and Flora unhesitatingly cut through the hound. It split in two, and gore spattered her face. She was panting with fear and horror.

Selena lay limp and weak. The king had stopped laughing, and was deadly silent.

'We have the sunsword,' said Pike. Flora, raised it above her head. 'And we have the hunting horn.' Simon pulled himself upright and showed it. 'And with them we will bring you down. You killed my father, the Knight of the Shark, a loyal man who would not do your hideous bidding. You killed many fathers, many mothers, brothers, sisters, friends. And all for nothing!'

Simon's leg was aching and bleeding from the hound's bite. He was ragged and torn, but he was there; his quest was so nearly finished. He lifted Selena up, and she leaned close into him.

'I am Simon Goldhawk,' he said, his voice ringing out into the square. 'I have the hunting horn. And I want my sister back.'

'I am Flora Williamson,' shouted Flora. 'I have the sunsword. And I want my brother.'

Selena coughed. Simon felt her shivering, but she pulled away from him, and faced her father across the square.

'I am the Silver Princess,' she shouted. There was a rustling of noise from the courtiers above, a shimmering of movement from the townspeople, and the king's shadow shook. 'And I call for the king's end!'

Simon put the hunting horn to his lips, and Flora brandished the sunsword. She could feel it singing to her, a melody sweet and powerful. It knew what it was about to do.

Pike grabbed a sword from the ground, and fell into a battle stance. Selena simply stood, gazing across at the man who had given her life, and who had taken it away from so many people.

The king advanced slowly. There was something strange about him – stranger than usual.

He was crying. Tears were pouring down his face.

'My child . . .' he was saying, over and over again. 'My daughter . . . My Lena . . .'

The Knight of the Swan barred his way. 'Go no further, my king.'

But the king passed him, and came within reach of Pike's arm.

His shadow fizzed, as if it could sense the presence of its destroyers.

'My Lena . . . My little one,' said the king, and kneeled on the stone slabs of the square, head bowed.

'Father . . .'

'Don't trust him,' hissed Pike.

Selena stretched out a hand, and her father reached out his in answer, and their fingers came closer and closer.

The Knight of the Swan kneeled on the ground too.

The king's fingers were almost touching Selena's, and then they were grasping hands and everything stopped.

There was a whooshing sound, of something coming through the air very fast, and Selena was on her back with an arrow sticking out of her leg. One of the king's guards yelled in triumph.

Simon scrambled to help Selena. She was pale and broken, and dark blood was pooling from the wound.

'No!' whispered Simon. 'No! This can't be happening . . .' He touched the arrow.

'Leave it in . . .' gasped Selena.

But now the king was back on his feet, and he knocked Pike over into Flora's arm, making her drop the sunsword as the Knight of the Swan reared up and grabbed the reins of her horse. Simon was trapped by two guards, whilst two more lifted up Selena. There was no sign of the Lady of the Stag.

'A pretty pass we've come to,' said the king, holding the sunsword. Its radiance dimmed. 'Such a beautiful thing, to be so deadly. The sheath please.'

Shaking with fury, Flora took the scabbard off her belt and handed it to the king, who looked longingly at the shining blade for a second more, before sheathing it.

The golden light went out, and the stark light of the Silver Kingdom crept back into their surroundings. The king handed the sunsword to Malek. Then he took the hunting horn and its baldrick from Simon's neck, and held it up, looking through it.

'So powerful,' he said. 'And yet so small. These are the two things that can break my shadow. And the Realm had them for so long before I hid them . . . Well, I have them back now. Bruin!'

Bruin came scuttling forwards, and took the horn from the king.

The king made a signal with his left hand. A

dozen guards marched up. Two grabbed Flora as she kicked and screamed, and Pike was surrounded.

The cart that Pike had brought drew up beside them. Sitting on it was a hooded figure.

Its outline prompted Pike to shake. Suddenly he was in his vision again, and he was also, confusingly, in the present moment. He realised the two were coming together, and his mind started to darken.

The king bent low and touched Flora on her forehead, and then did the same to Simon. They both dropped their heads, their necks drooping, and a film seemed to go over their eyes.

'No!' shouted Pike. But the king was touching Selena's forehead too, and then the three of them were being bundled into the cart.

'Why not me?' sobbed Pike. 'Why not me? What have you done to them?'

'I have other plans for you, son of a traitor,' whispered the king. 'Now, take them to the palace!'

The figure on the cart pulled back its hood. Andaria. And Pike knew that now all was lost.

Chapter Twenty-One

THE SHATTERED
STATUE

T HE CART TRUNDLED slowly towards the
black gates of the palace, wheels creaking, the
hooves of the horned horse ringing and echoing on
the stone. The courtiers were still thronging the
balconies, watching in silence – because of wonder,
or terror, or both, Pike could not tell. Bound by the
guards, he sat crouched helplessly in-between the
limp bodies of his friends; Princess Selena lay like a
rag doll opposite him.

The hope of our kingdom, thought Pike, *all in tatters.
My vision. It came true. Why didn't I see it coming? Why
didn't I stop it?* He cursed himself and bit his lip,

rubbing his bonds, but they were too tight. *No, no, no*, he thought. *This can't be happening.*

They passed the platform where the king had been standing, and Pike saw the Blessed Ones. There was the little girl, Anna, Simon's sister, weeping and trying to run off the edge to her brother. Flora's brother, Johnny, was holding her back. Her coronet was tilted and her long dress was rumpled. Johnny's face was pale and drawn, his silver cheekbone catching the light. The little monkey creatures were capering and chattering, and they hissed at Pike as the cart went past.

Pike was desolate. If the Silver Princess died, then that meant there was nobody who would dare take on the king – certainly not her half-sisters. And if Flora and Simon were out of action, the sunsword and the hunting horn could do no harm to the king. The sight of his friends, lying there empty, was too much for Pike. *My kingdom, my family, my friends all ruined*, he thought. *And there's nothing I can do about it.* He tried not to think about what the king meant by 'other plans' for him.

He looked around. Andaria, the green rider, drove the cart – her cool, hard eyes staring ahead. The king was dancing in the square. The Knight of the Swan was being tended to by a servant, who was bandaging up his eye. Soldiers were everywhere and courtiers were watching. Bruin and Malek stood at the palace gates.

'My lords!' Pike shouted up to the courtiers. 'Help us!'

Was there a rustle on the balconies? Some movement? He couldn't tell. Where was the Lady of the Stag? Where were Scarlet and Eagret? *I must be able to escape somehow*, he thought. *Come on.*

He kicked Simon, but Simon did not respond.

The gates of the palace loomed ahead. Andaria brought the cart to a halt. Guards appeared. The royal hounds barked and slavered, their scales glinting, their teeth bared, their hideous, bloodshot eyes glaring.

The king twirled his way towards the entrance of the palace.

'More people to be Taken Apart,' he said, looking up at the trees surrounding the square, where the remains of all those that had gone before hung. 'You, though, son of a traitor, will suffer a different fate. You will watch your friends die. And then you will be left to starve in the square . . .'

A speck in the sky, golden and strange, was coming towards them.

The king didn't stop dancing from foot to foot, but the guards paused. The courtiers set up a furious whispering, and the townspeople began to creep back into the square.

'A nothing,' said the king, spinning round, his arms out like a dervish.

But the golden speck was getting bigger, and moving slowly towards them.

Pike's eyes widened in amazement. The golden shape was clearer now, and hovering above the statue in the centre of the square. When he realised what it was, he gasped, and his heart leaped with joy.

It was Hover, in his form as a winged man, his peacock feathers beating and keeping him level.

Noise was everywhere, a buzz of chatter and shouts from the balconies, people leaning out and calling to each other. The people in the square gasped, whispering, *'When man shall fly, the worlds will die . . .'*

'No,' said the king. 'It is not there.'

Hover descended to the top of the statue of Silvanus and his feet caught the tip of the crown. It fell to the ground and shattered. He swooped to the cart, and with the tips of his wings caressed the heads of Simon, Flora and the princess.

'It is an illusion,' said the king. 'The shattered statue . . . Dance, my people, dance!'

Pike made a renewed effort with his bonds.

Hover settled on top of the statue. An archer shot at him but he caught and snapped the arrow in his hand with one movement.

'The worlds shall die!' came a familiar voice, and the Lady of the Stag strode through the people in the square, flanked by Scarlet and Eagret and followed by those rebels who remained.

'A nothing,' said the king, 'a story, an illusion . . . For babes, a story, coming to life! We know it cannot be true.'

'What's going on?' said someone, and Pike, startled, looked away from Hover and saw that Simon was waking up. 'I felt something, like the bird-deer . . .'

There was a groan and Flora sat up. 'I feel like I've got a hangover,' she said. 'Have I?' Then she glanced around and her face fell. 'No, still here . . .'

Selena sat up with sudden movement. Her shoulder was aching; she held a hand to her leg and felt the blood, sticky and warm. She felt faint. She didn't know if she had much time left. There was an important message she had to deliver. She had to do it now. 'I have something to tell you . . .' she said.

Andaria leaped up, her long green cloak flowing behind her. She grabbed a spear from the nearest guard and hurled it at Hover, yelling. It rebounded off him and clattered uselessly on the stone. The little monkey creatures swarmed up the statue and started pawing at the air beneath Hover's feet. His wings shimmered and fluttered.

Simon thought he looked like an angel. Whatever an angel really was.

Flora ripped at her bonds with her teeth. 'Harder than it looks,' she said ruefully, tearing them in two with a great tug. She quickly set about releasing the others.

'I say we do it now,' said Flora. 'We get the sunsword and the hunting horn, capture the king, free Johnny and Anna, and go home! We'll be having Marmite on toast before you know it . . .'

'It's the only way,' agreed Simon. 'There's no time to think. Just do it.'

All around them was turmoil and confusion. The people had rushed into the square; none dared to attack the guards, but there was a tension in their movements. Some of the courtiers and knights had come down from their balconies, and were mingling amongst the townspeople – there was a woman in dark blue armour with a crested helm on her head like a falcon; somewhere else a young girl squire in a black and white jerkin. Everyone was whispering, talking, moving about. It was difficult to focus. Simon suddenly realised how hungry he was, and how tired.

And then he saw Anna, standing on the edge of the platform, chained to the throne with Johnny, and courage began to edge its way back into his heart.

'An outrage!' yelled the Knight of the Swan at Hover. 'This is a direct attack. Take him prisoner, immediately, and we will retaliate against the Golden Realm!'

The guards ran to the statue and circled it, threatening with their spikes, but unsure what to do. The knight held the bandage to his eye and swore.

The king had gone to stand beneath the statue, and was tilting his head from side to side, squinting upwards. There was a circle of guards around him and the Knight of the Swan stood outside it, sword drawn, ready to protect his master.

'What are you doing here, emissary of the Realm? How do you dare to enter here?' said the king.

Hover said nothing, but alighted on the statue's

head, and the two little monkey creatures scampered down away from him, hissing and yelping, as if they'd been burned. They sheltered under the ridge of the platform and peeped out, chattering.

Pike looked around. Bruin and Malek were standing next to each other, Bruin looking on with the horn, Malek cradling the sunsword. Pike jumped out of the cart, and Flora landed firmly beside him. Simon helped Selena down. She limped awkwardly. Simon ripped off an arm from his peasant top and tied it quickly around Selena's wound.

'Watch the prisoners!' shouted a guard, who rushed clumsily at them.

'Don't come near us,' Pike said, and kicked him in the stomach, knocking him over and taking his sword. Another soldier swung at him with a spear but Simon blocked it and used the momentum to kick him off balance.

'You go for Malek,' said Simon to Flora. 'I'll go for Bruin.'

The giant was gazing impassively up at Hover, the horn hanging from his left hand.

Simon ran for it. He ran in the knowledge that what he was doing was crazy, and that he had no hope against the giant, except born of surprise. He charged up to Bruin from the side, and wrenched at the horn.

The giant, as if troubled by a fly, looked down and saw Simon. There was a moment of unbearable tension as Simon felt the pull of the giant's muscles. He looked into the giant's eyes and saw a terrible, quiet rage, and pain both deep and ancient.

'Please,' Simon begged under his breath. 'Please.'

He felt the strap tighten.

And then it loosened, and Simon was holding the horn in his hand, and Bruin's eyes were signalling to Simon. 'Do it,' they said.

Startled, Simon paused for second, and he understood. The giant was a prisoner too.

At a nod from Bruin, the dwarf Malek slipped the sunsword into Flora's hands.

'It must be a trap,' she said, looking at Simon.

'Take it!' hissed Simon.

Malek smiled and bowed. Flora took the sunsword, open-mouthed.

Flora and Simon faced each other. All around them the crowds were looking at Hover and the king, and everyone was shouting and bustling. There was a kind of madness in the air. More of the knights had come down into the square, and their armour and helmets and glittering clothes merged with the people.

'This is it,' said Simon to Flora.

She nodded, her mouth set, her hair long and plastered against her face, her eyes full of fire. 'When I say go,' said Flora. 'We go.'

They heard the king laughing, saw Hover swooping.

'Three . . . two . . . one . . . Go!'

Flora unsheathed the sunsword, and Simon blew a note of warning. The glow from the sword spread out across the square, and the low sound of the horn burrowed into everybody's minds. Everybody swung round; every eye was focused on Simon and Flora, and silence washed through the air.

Only the king remained with his back to them, staring up at Hover.

The sun was in Simon's eyes, and the king's silhouette looked like a devil.

Time seemed to be moving differently, like a wave, rolling them onwards. The sunsword's glow poured over everything, imbuing it with golden, beautiful light. Flora felt its beauty and energy rushing through her. And its deadliness. The people made a way for them as they passed, shrinking back from the blade.

As Simon and Flora edged closer to the king,

he turned and grinned, his eyes red, and he bit his tongue between his teeth.

The Knight of the Swan threw himself in front of the king. His helmet was off, and his black hair framed his white face, his eye obviously paining him. He looked panicked, confused – something Simon thought was impossible. Above them a swan flew by.

'Sir Mark,' said Simon. 'You can't stand against the hunting horn and the sunsword. Either the sunsword kills you, or I'll blow the note of death, and you'll be no more of this world.'

'He is my king,' said the knight. 'And I would die willingly for him.'

The king clapped his hands, and the knight went for Simon. He was swift and practised.

Flora jumped to defend Simon, and the knight's sword cut into her left arm. The energy of the sunsword was so powerful in her that she did not feel it, though she saw the blood dripping down.

The Knight of the Swan looked furious and desperate. 'I told you,' he said. 'It did not have to be like this.'

Simon put the horn to his lips. Flora readied the sunsword.

'You are children,' said the knight. 'You have not

seen what I have seen.' Around them the people roared, a multitude of voices, a deafening din. Hover dived overhead. Andaria marched towards them, green cloak billowing. Anna and Johnny shouted encouragement.

'I've never killed anyone,' said Flora.

'Then don't start with me,' said the knight. He raised his sword. 'I warn you.'

Flora rushed at the knight and slammed the sunsword into his blade. It was was cut clean in half, and the knight stared at the stump. That moment of hesitation was enough for Simon to deal him a blow on the head, which knocked him backwards.

Now Simon and Flora were facing the king, close enough to reach out and touch him. His face was drawn, stretched. His eyes were extraordinary – they gleamed with a red glow. His shadow buzzed and shimmered around him.

'None has ever reached me,' said the king. 'I dream . . .' He swayed from side to side, his sharp horns glinting. 'I dream of things that are broken . . . That is my name, in your world, in theirs. They say that I am broken. But everything is,' he hissed. 'Everything is broken . . . The shattered spear, the worlds torn apart . . . The mare is hobbled, the eagle clipped, the mother lies dying . . .'

'Do it!' yelled Simon. The horn's power was throbbing through his cells, urging him to blow it. He felt it enter his mind, clutching at him, forming the only possibility that it could: death and destruction.

Flora drew back the sunsword, its golden energy surging through her. Hover swooped low from the statue. Andaria was mere paces away, stalking up slowly behind Simon and Flora.

Tense, frightened, and yet filled with courage, Flora held the sunsword above her head. Simon put the hunting horn to his lips.

'One,' he said. 'Two . . .'

He was about to blow, and Flora was swinging the sunsword down on to the king's shadow when Selena cried out, 'Stop!'

Flora, confused, swung round, and lowered the sword.

'I have to tell you something!' called Selena. 'Stop! Stop!'

'Why?' yelled Simon, anger coursing through him.

'You musn't do it. The energy is too much. If you do it, you'll die! Both of you! You'll both die!'

Chapter Twenty-Two

THE SHADOW
FALLS

THE KING'S GAZE flickered, he bowed his head, and grinned.

'It's true,' he said. Then he gathered himself to his full height. 'It seems, Simon, Flora, my daughter, my dearest friends, that you cannot win. I want Bruin and Malek Taken Apart at once, traitors both. I thank you, my dearest Knight of the Swan, for your loyalty.'

Anna, standing on the edge of the platform, burst into tears, and rattled and banged her chains with Johnny. Hover came to a pause on the statue once more.

'No!' shouted Simon. 'We will bring you down!'

'No! Don't! Don't die and leave me here!' called Anna.

Johnny joined in. 'Flora! Don't do it! Stay here with me – we'll find another way to escape!'

The king was within reach of Flora and Simon. All it would take was one slash of the sunsword, and one blow of the hunting horn, and the king's shadow would be split open, and he would be at their mercy.

But they would also die.

'I don't believe you!' shouted Flora.

Selena was hobbling towards them. Her lips were dry and cracked, and her voice was weak.

'It's true,' she said. 'Believe me. I knew it. I've always known it.'

'Why didn't you tell us?' said Simon, aghast.

'Of course she wouldn't tell you,' said the king. 'She was using you – little pawns to be sacrificed for the greater kill.' He grinned, his red tongue poking out between his teeth, eyes gleaming. His protective shadow buzzed and slipped around him.

'I cannot let Simon and Flora die,' said Selena. 'Even if it means . . .'

'That I continue to rule?' snarled the king. 'What a bind you are in!'

Selena suddenly filled with anger and screamed, 'You would kill us anyway! I can't bear it!' She was shivering, a wreck.

Simon thought deeply. He thought about the journey that he had come on. He remembered golden light filtering through the trees. He remembered Anna, jumping up and down. A vase breaking. Shadows, slippery. A knight at the doors of the British Museum. A chase, swans beating through the dark. He thought about the blackness at the centre of the worlds. He thought about Hover, and what he had been about to reveal in the cave.

He thought about all these things.

I am whole, he thought, *a whole person. But there are many more such people here than there are of me. Anna . . . She can go through on her own. Johnny will look after her, and Flora too. And my parents will have her back. And I . . . I will make my choice.*

The decision was forming, and it had the shape of a blade.

I can't let these people continue like this. What is my own life worth against all of theirs?

He heard Anna, and thought of his father and mother lying in bed asleep, not knowing at all what was happening to them both. 'If I do it,' he said to

Selena, 'will you make sure that Anna gets back safely?' He took the black shadow-sphere from his pocket and gave it to the princess. A tear rolled down her cheek as she nodded.

'Flora,' said Simon. 'Give me the sword.'

When Flora spoke her voice was strange. 'No, Simon.'

'What? Give it to me, Flora.'

The king laughed. 'Children, children . . .'

Flora ignored him. 'Simon, we have to do this together. This is our destiny. We must save them . . . even if it means death.' There were tears sparkling in her eyes.

Simon held Flora to his chest, and for a moment everything was still.

Then, without speaking, they parted, and Simon began to blow the note of death, Flora hoisted the sunsword, and the king's expression became a mask of laughing glee, and Johnny cried out and Anna sobbed.

In a sudden movement, Andaria jumped in front of Simon and Flora, and snatched the sunsword from Flora and the horn from Simon. She turned to face the king.

'No!' yelled Simon. He raged, incandescent. 'No! Not now, you can't!'

Flora ran to Andaria, but the rider turned and hissed, holding the sunsword at Flora's breast. She pulled her hood down, revealing her face, and there she stood, a tall girl of about twenty, with wild brown hair and eyes that glared hard.

She spat on to the stone. 'Do you not recognise me, Selenus?'

Her voice reminded Simon of something.

The king looked at her intently.

'You will address me properly. You are Andaria, my servant,' said the king.

'Do you not recognise me?' she said again, her accent becoming more and more familiar to Simon. She thrust her face into the king's.

The king stepped back from her.

'Kill her too,' he said, as the Knight of the Swan struggled to his feet.

'I have been waiting for so long. I have been so close, waiting, waiting for this moment. I never dreamed it would come. But when those children came through . . . I knew it. I knew it was my chance. The shadow falls, my king,' said Andaria. The sunsword made her face glow. She bowed, formally. And she slashed at the king's shadow.

There was a terrible ripping sound and everyone

put their hands to their ears. The king screamed in fury. 'What is this? This cannot be happening. You are of the Kingdom! You cannot slay me.'

'That, Selenus, is where you are wrong. Do you remember the names of the children you took over the years? How many was it?'

'What mean you, servant?' said the king.

'Do you remember a girl who was five years old, whose brother wished her away? Who came, terrified and wailing, into the halls of your palace, and who you fed on? Who you kept for seven straight years in the black prison, until she was nearly dead? Do you remember a girl called Harriet Fielding? She was the one. She was the one who escaped. She didn't die, torn apart by hounds. She escaped, and lived in the forest, on wild things, half-alive. And all the time she nourished revenge in her heart.

'I have nothing. I have nobody. Nobody will mourn me, nobody will miss me. And so I, Harriet Fielding, known in the Kingdom as Andaria, am become the slayer of the Broken King!' She put the hunting horn to her lips, and blew the note of death. And Simon recognised her voice now – faint, but there all the same: the safe, normal tones of a London accent, but filled with rage and fury.

The gap in the king's shadow widened, and then it slipped off the king's body. He appeared without it, ancient and wizened. Andaria struck him with the sunsword, and then ran him through.

The shadow fluttered and buzzed, and the sunsword flamed, and the horn's blast echoed and once more there seemed to be a tear in the very nature of things.

'The Way has been opened,' called Hover.

The king's younger form struggled back through the surface of his ancient body as he summoned his last reserves of power. He was smiling. 'Andaria,' he said. 'There was always something strange about you . . .' Black, smokey coils reached out from his body and grappled her, but she did not struggle.

'Go back!' called Andaria to Simon and Flora. 'Go back with your brother and sister. Return to the home that I barely knew, and give my parents this.' She threw something at them. Simon caught it reflexively. It was a little charm bracelet.

'I have prepared for this day,' said the king. And indeed, the world seemed to be shaking. 'My shadow . . . my shadow from the centre of the worlds . . . the mare is hobbled, the eagle clipped, the mother lies dying . . .'

A golden glow appeared in the south, and Hover swooped exultantly. 'They come!'

'The trap is sprung,' laughed the king, pulling Andaria towards him. Andaria let out a huge sigh, and fell limp into his arms. He thrust her aside, and she collapsed to the ground. Her face was white and strained, her lips blue. The edges of the king's body were blurring, and his face was wavering in and out of focus.

'Look!' called Simon. From the south a great golden mass was advancing in the sky. It moved swiftly, and it filled Simon's heart with joy.

The king laughed once more, high and weird, and there was a great rushing noise, as of something tearing in the very fabric of the universe, and the king vanished from sight, pulling Andaria with him.

There was silence, apart from the beating of wings.

Stillness bloomed out from where the king had stood.

The Knight of the Swan pulled himself to his feet. He looked worn, exhausted, but there was still an air of pride in his features. His cheeks were hollow and his remaining eye glinted oddly. A swan flew down and settled next to him, and he put his hand on the swan's head. The swan seemed to nuzzle him for a moment.

The knight said, 'I served my king. I swore an oath. I was loyal. Never let it be said otherwise.'

And he kneeled down, took the locket off his neck, kissed it, laid it gently down on the ground, and ran himself through with his sword.

Silence, spreading from the wound.

Blood, seeping on the stone.

Tears, flowing in the crowd.

Confusion.

Light.

A swan, beating its wings, flying off into the sky.

Slowly, Simon went to the knight. He was lying lifeless, pale, looking small now. Simon kneeled by him. *You were true*, he thought. *You were wicked, and a murderer, but you were true to your king*. Simon picked up the locket and opened it. Inside it was a lock of hair. Simon, wondering if the knight had had a sweetheart somewhere, put the locket into his pocket, swearing to himself to return it to that person.

And then the stillness retreated. Somebody coughed, and then somebody clapped, and then, as if by some command, every single person in the square was yelling, laughing, shouting and cheering. The noise was deafening. Simon, dizzied, was surrounded by a surge of gleeful men and women. The king's guards put down their weapons; the royal hounds lay with their heads on their paws, slavering quietly. Their master had gone.

Slowly but surely, the soldiers and the people met together. For a moment, it looked like there would be a fight.

And then a wonderful thing happened.

'My son . . .' called someone, and an old lady came pushing out from the crowd and ran towards the soldiers. One of them took his helmet off, held his arms out, and kneeled on the ground.

'My son!' The old lady kissed the top of her son's head. And then all the soldiers took their helmets off, and hurled them on to the ground. Metal clanging on stone.

Somebody picked up Flora and put her on his shoulders. Simon found himself hoisted up between two people, and Pike was lifted up too. Someone brought a chair for Selena, and bore it to the platform where the Blessed Ones stood as somebody struck off their chains.

Simon leaped joyfully to the platform.

And suddenly he was holding a ball of sobbing joy.

He embraced Anna, and a huge sense of relief, as

strong and powerful as a wind, rushed through him, and almost made him falter. But he stayed strong, and held his sister, and whispered into her ear, 'Anna, I'm sorry. I'm so sorry. I love you. I've come to take you back. We'll be home soon, don't you worry. All we have to do is go to the stone and then we'll be eating chocolate and watching TV. And I don't even mind about the broken music player.'

'Simon . . .' said Anna. 'I miss Mummy and Daddy so much . . .'

'I know, I know . . .' he whispered, and kissed her on the top of her head.

Meanwhile, Johnny had run to Flora and was enveloping her in an enormous bear hug.

'I'll change,' he was saying. 'I'll change . . . This has made me realise things . . . I was an idiot, an arrogant idiot.'

Flora couldn't say anything, but wept and wept.

The light and the rushing of wings became stronger. Above them was a host of men and women riding on bird-deer, golden wings spreading and soaring, their expressions joyful as they landed and circled the square, coming to a halt before the statue.

There, on the lead bird-deer, was Mithras, and he was calm and shining. Behind him were Raven, Cautes and Cautopates. And Pike was suddenly running, for there was his mother, dismounting, and they embraced.

Selena took to the platform, followed by the Lady of the Stag and her supporters. Stumbling, she clutched her shoulder, and the Lady of the Stag held her up, but Selena pushed her help away, and stood unaided. She took a deep breath, before shouting, 'My people!'

There was a great roar of approval, and hats and helmets went up into the air.

'Too long have you suffered under a tyrant king. We have fought against him, with Mithras of the Golden Realm!'

The crowd yelled his name, and Mithras bowed.

'With the children of the ones Taken Apart!'

Eagret, Scarlet and the others stood on the platform, bloodied but unbowed, and the square resounded with joy.

'And Pike, son of the Knight of the Shark and the Lady of the Snake, who risked his life to go to the place in-between and fetch the slayers of the king! Flora Williamson and Simon Goldhawk!'

But we didn't kill him, thought Simon. He released Anna, and he and Flora went to Selena.

Simon spoke haltingly. Everybody was quiet. 'We did what we could,' he said. 'We were punished for what we did in our world, and we were thrown into this quest. But it was Andaria, the green rider, who stopped the king in the end. We should remember her.'

'In memory of Andaria, this day will be named after her,' said Selena.

The Lady of the Stag yelled out, 'I declare Princess Selena Queen of the Silver Kingdom. All in favour!'

The cheer of assent was deafening.

The new queen, smiling, strode in front of the Lady of the Stag and held her arms up in a gesture of triumph.

And a strange thing happened: from out of either side of Selena's head began to grow two horns, straight out, then curving a little, silvery and fine. And when they had finished growing, the queen bowed her head and said, 'I will serve you well, my people. The long, terrible reign of my father is over. Consider yourselves free.'

Four knights came with a palanquin, placed her gently into it, and took her into the palace.

'Now,' said the Lady of the Stag, turning to Simon, Flora, Anna and Johnny while the people around them started to sing a song of celebration as they tore down the portraits of the king, 'let's get you all home.'

Chapter Twenty-Three

THE WORLDS
SHALL DIE

THEY PASSED THE rest of the day in the palace, simply enjoying each other's company. As their wounds were seen to, Simon told Anna the story of how they'd got to the Kingdom, and relived each moment as he told it. Already, though, it felt like a dream, as if it had passed away into legend. Time seemed to be slipping away from him, and rushing him towards home. *Soon this will all be nothing but a memory*, he thought.

Flora rummaged in the sack that held all their belongings, and pulled out Johnny's leather jacket.

'Here,' she said shyly.

He took it without saying anything, and automatically felt in the pockets. They were empty. He looked at Flora, and there was a world of sorrow in his eyes. She held out the syringe, from where she'd been hiding it in her hand.

'It helped us, you know. I wouldn't have been able to come here without it. We needed something of yours.'

He held out his hand, as if to take it. And then he dropped it.

'Keep it,' he said. 'Keep it as a reminder. I want to know that you've got it, and I want to know that I will never need it again.'

She kissed him, and her tears wet the shoulder of his jacket.

All around them the people caroused: they wore flowers in their hair, and the knights and the people danced together as Mithras and those from the Golden Realm looked on.

The Lady of the Stag came to them as night fell. 'The queen is rested,' she said. 'She has been tended to by the healers, and her wound is staunched. Her shoulder is being reset. She wishes now to see you off home.'

They went out and joined Selena at the palace gates. She was flanked by Clara and several knights.

When she came out, the entire square fell silent. The royal hounds were gone; the chittering monkey creatures had scuttled off. Her shoulder was strapped up in a sling the same colour as her silver dress. On her head she wore a silver tiara with a single emerald in it. While her horns were clear on either side of her head, they did not look frightening. *They're part of her,* thought Simon. *The moon. She is the moon, somehow.*

'Let us go!' she cried. 'I shall take the Blessed Ones and their siblings back to the standing stone, so they can return to their homes.'

Warmth filled Simon's heart, and he hugged Anna, who hadn't left his side all the time.

'The Way is open now! We can send all of you back to where you came from! And things will be like they once were . . .'

'For them,' whispered Simon to Flora. 'But not for us. We'll go back to our world, and it will be the same old stuff, school and exams and wet holidays . . . I'd love to be on the beach in the rain, though, wouldn't you, Anna?'

His sister giggled and tickled him.

Another thought came into Simon's head, of the three circles in the cave, and the blackness where they met. *I've seen what is strange and other . . . and I will remember it always. And yet I haven't seen the Golden Realm,* he thought, with a pang. *I bet it's beautiful.*

The way Anna was twisting her hair jerked him out of his thoughts. He squeezed her shoulder fondly.

A harsh voice came from the side of the square, and there was a commotion in the crowd. Somebody was pushing through the people, knocking them out of the way, and not keeping very quiet about it at all.

A man arrived, panting, at the foot of the platform where stood Selena and the others.

'No! They can't go! Not those two!' he panted. 'I want compensation!'

'What is it?' said the queen gently. Simon's stomach contracted.

'These two here! They – don't know what they did to me, but knocked me out hard! Was going to get some crescents for them!'

Simon, relieved, almost laughed. It was the carter, the silver-haired man that he'd accidentally laid out with the hunting horn.

'I'm sorry,' Simon said to the queen. 'We had a small . . . accident with this man.'

'Accident! Woke up in the freezing cold I did, had to limp all the way home – stole my cart and goods and everything, they did . . .'

The queen raised her hand and said, 'We will find you compensation, for your cart, your produce and your crescents.' She motioned to an attendant, who led the still grumbling carter away.

'Well, I'm glad he's all right at least,' said Flora in an undertone, and Simon, smiling, agreed.

'There are many things to settle,' continued the queen. 'We have all committed crimes under the reign of my father. There will be an investigation.' She looked sorrowful. 'But we will repair ourselves, and we will grow, and we will once again become the Kingdom that we have been.'

There was a moment of silence as the people considered the past. Then the queen lifted her head and smiled. 'Now it is time to go.'

And they went, the queen leading as Simon and Anna, Flora and Johnny walked four abreast, slowly through the crowds, who threw kisses and shook their hands and grinned at them as they went.

Ahead of them was Eagret, spinning around with a garland of flowers on her head. Scarlet, with a magehawk on her shoulder, was dancing with a young squire whose tunic was embroidered with spiders. 'Goodbye!' they called. 'Goodbye! May the Threefold Goddess be with you!' Scarlet released the squire, came towards them, and grabbed Pike, giving him a kiss on the cheek before letting him go and running back into the crowd. Pike, too startled to react, merely blushed, but he caught her eye as she waved to him. He raised a hand in reply.

'Be lucky!' called various people in the crowd.

Simon looked back at the palace, and saw the giant Bruin peering out from a window beside the dwarf Malek. *They will be punished*, he thought . . . *but they will not be killed*.

When they reached the standing stone, the embassy from the Golden Realm was waiting there.

Simon felt anger return, boiling in his stomach, and he was about to say something. But Mithras smiled, opened his arms wide, and came towards them, enveloping Simon and Flora. His touch was warm and strengthening and Simon felt golden power flowing through his limbs.

'You made us puppets,' he whispered.

Mithras released him and held him at arm's length. Raven came to join them, her long black hair flowing in the breeze, with the two Cats – Cautes and Cautopates – who winked at Flora.

'Simon,' said Mithras, 'the will was in you already. You felt those things about Anna. You wanted her to leave, you hated her in that moment. And you are right. This quest was a punishment, in many ways. They always are. But there are other reasons why we chose you. Your bravery, your strength and your kindness. The pair of you performed all those terrible tasks. And you were willing to give away your lives to save more.'

Simon nodded. 'I think I understand. There was so much at stake . . .' *A whole kingdom*, he thought, *resting on us.*

'Do you forgive us, Simon?' said Mithras.

Simon shook his head. 'No. I don't. But I know what you had to do. And I am pleased that we played a part in it.'

'That is right fair,' said Mithras gently.

'And we couldn't have done it without Pike,' said Flora, and then Pike stepped forward, and the three of them hugged each other tightly.

'He will be rewarded in due course,' said the queen, smiling. Pike looked at his feet and blushed once more. 'For now, do you please kneel before me.'

Pike stumbled a little, glancing awkwardly at Simon and Flora, then felt a swell of pride and kneeled, bowing his head before the queen. One of her attendants placed a garland of sweet white flowers around his neck. Another handed the queen a jewelled sword. 'I create you Knight of the Shark,' cried the queen, touching him lightly on each shoulder. 'Loyal subject, your lands will be reinstated and your fortunes restored.'

Feeling a little overwhelmed, Pike, the new Knight of the Shark, rose steadily to his feet, and the queen grasped his hand and raised it into the air. Simon and Flora joined in the cheering, clapping and whooping. Scarlet cupped her hands together around her mouth and hurrahed, and Pike caught her eye and held her gaze.

The queen spoke. 'Simon Goldhawk and Flora Williamson, the two from the place in-between. As your reward, you may keep the hunting horn and the sunsword. You will always be honoured in the Silver Kingdom and the Golden Realm, where the bards will sing of Flora of the Sunsword, Simon of the Hunting Horn, and Pike, the Knight of the Shark. And they will sing of the green rider Andaria, who was Harriet Fielding when taken by my father. In her memory we keep silence for a moment.'

Simon held Anna tightly and kissed her forehead. In the silence he remembered Andaria, her burning revenge, her bravery.

Torches shimmered, magehawks dived overhead, and Anna snuffled and wiped her nose.

'And now, let us proceed! The Way is open, but we will, to remember my father and his terror, perform the three tasks. Are you ready?' The queen spoke gladly, her voice full of joy.

Anna sniffed, and the queen turned to look at her. 'What's the matter?' said the queen gently.

'It's . . .' She put out her hands; they glinted silver.

'Come here,' said Mithras. 'You too, Johnny.'

The two approached Mithras. 'Simon,' he said gravely. 'Do you have the skin-map?'

The skin-map. Simon had forgotten all about it. 'It's in the sack, with everything else . . .'

Pike had it; he gave it to Simon, who dug into it and pulled out the scroll. Simon handed it reverently to Mithras.

Mithras took it, made a sign above it, and then touched Johnny's cheek gently, before doing the same to Anna's hands. The skin-map unrolled in his hands, and then it came apart. The pieces started to crawl down his arms towards Johnny and Anna.

Anna gasped, and Johnny yelped with pain as the silver on his cheek shimmered; the bits of skin reached his face, stretched, then grew back over his cheekbone. Within a second he was touching his new skin, a broad grin on his face. Anna felt a burning sensation in her hands and started to wail, but soon enough it had gone, and she was looking down at her very own fingers as they had been. She was so startled by them that she hugged Mithras.

The four of them faced the standing stone. Simon grasped Anna's hand; Flora grabbed Johnny's waist. Flora and Simon took out the black shadow-spheres, opening them and holding them out.

'Take one,' he whispered to Anna.

'I just want a glass of milk,' said Flora. 'Real milk.'

'I want my bed . . .' groaned Johnny as he took one from Flora. 'My duvet . . . My records! My philosophy books . . . I've got some new thoughts about all that now . . .'

'Ready?' said Simon, lifting up the hunting horn and blowing a note.

There was a strange ripping sound. Mithras looked up sharply. 'Wait . . .' he said. A tear appeared in the air above the standing stone, as if it was a curtain and behind it was another stage. There was a rumbling in the background, as of thunder in the distance.

Simon felt the thrill of home rushing through him. He held Anna's hand tightly. There were trees through the gap, and the sun shining on a world that he knew, a world that he still had to get to know. He turned towards the queen. The thundering was louder now.

'I . . . I don't know what to say,' he said.

'Go,' said the queen. 'With the blessing of both realms.'

Simon smiled at the queen, and Flora began to unsheath the sunsword.

'Wait!'

It was Mithras, striding towards the gap. 'No! Don't go through! Something's wrong!'

The thundering sound was terrible, and the ground seemed to tremble. Through the gap everything was rushing, changing. One moment they could see the trees and greenery of the clearing in the south of England, the next there was a golden glow, and then there was a terrible blackness.

A wind came out of the gap, so strong that it blew over the queen's palanquin; dresses billowed backwards, and Simon, Flora, Johnny and Anna were pushed away.

'Hold on to me!' Simon clamped his hand over Anna's wrist.

'What's going on?' shouted Flora over the noise.

'I don't know!'

A shape formed in the gap. A man, tall and robed, and on his head a pair of horns.

'The king!' someone screamed. 'How can it be?'

'No, it's not him, it's an image of him,' said Mithras.

The image of the king laughed, smoke and blackness swirling around him.

'I have set a trap,' he said. 'Anyone who tries to cross between the worlds will die.' A horrible smile lit up his face, and he bowed low. 'The centre begins to crumble . . .' The image shimmered, and vanished.

'Close the gap! Close it before anything gets out!' shouted Mithras.

Through the gap now were deserts, wastelands, then vast oceans and red plains, icy mountains and blackness, a terrible, eternal void.

The void around the worlds.

'I don't know how!' called Selena.

The wind was rising. Johnny, Flora and Simon stood with their arms around Anna.

The queen struggled towards the gap with Mithras, Raven and the others. They locked hands. 'Perform the closing ritual!'

They chanted and danced and made signs in the air. But the wind still blew. 'It's not strong enough! More power!' called Mithras.

Energy poured from the small group, a silver glow from the queen mingling with a golden light from the people of the Realm. It all merged together into a surging mass, which forced its way to the gap, and drew the edges of the tear together.

The wind stopped. Everything fell flat. Mithras was pale and exhausted; Raven, panting, slid to the ground; the two Cats fainted. The queen collapsed, once more looking frail. 'Send magehawks to the holding places,' she croaked, and Clara whistled. Four birds appeared, black and shimmering, and at a whispered command they vanished into the shadows. 'Who has the talent? Who can use their animals to go between worlds? Send for those who can! The Knight of the Hawk . . .' Her voice was fading. 'Send to the priests of Boreas . . .'

Anna started to cry, huge drops that fell to the dusty ground like rain.

'What's the matter? What's happening?' asked Johnny frantically. He was scratching his arms inside the jacket, and his eyes were staring and bright.

'The king set a trap,' replied Selena, fitfully. 'He must have harmed the goddess in some way . . . The prophecy will come true. The worlds shall die.'

'The worlds shall die . . .' repeated Flora, thinking of her house, her mother sitting on the sofa with a wine glass in her hand, the television on; her father off somewhere . . . 'Oh, Johnny, I can't bear it . . .'

'There must be a way to stop him, there must be,' said Johnny insistently. 'All this time we've been chained up, and now we're almost free, and we can't do anything . . . '

Mithras spoke up. 'There is a way to stop this,' he said quietly. 'But it is full of danger. And to set this right, someone will need to go into the very heart of the worlds themselves.'

'The place where the circles meet,' said Simon, remembering the picture on the wall in the temple cave. 'But there's nothing there.'

'There is,' said Mithras. 'The abode of the goddess. The king has done something to it, and we must find out what that is. Otherwise, not only will you not be able to go home, but our worlds will begin to fade and crumble.'

'Ours too?' said Anna.

'Yours too,' said Mithras.

Simon wanted to scream, to pour his heart out, to beat his head against the ground. The wickedness of the king was overwhelming.

But he didn't.

'I know what you're going to say,' said Flora, catching his eye.

'And I'm with you too,' said Johnny.

'Anna,' said Simon quietly. 'The three of us are going to go on a journey . . .'

'You're not leaving me,' she said. 'I'm not staying here. I'm small — I can climb through things other people can't. You might need me.' She grabbed Simon, and he hugged her as tightly as he'd ever done.

'You're not going,' said Simon firmly. He stopped hugging her and held her by the hand. 'The three of us will do it,' said Simon. 'We will go to the centre of the worlds, and we will find out what the king has done, and we will put it right.'

'And you're not going without me,' said Pike.

'Well said, Knight of the Shark,' said Simon, and grasped hands with Pike, and Flora put her hand on top of theirs, joining Johnny too.

'The journey will be difficult,' said Mithras. 'You will need a guide. I must stay here and shore up what I can.'

'Then I will go with them too,' said Cautes.

'People from each world. That is good,' said Mithras.

'Then first we shall rest,' said the queen. 'Send magehawks to examine the Kingdom and bring the news. At any sign of decay, I must be informed immediately. Let us go to the palace. We shall see if we can communicate with the Golden Realm.'

It was a subdued group that made its way back to the city. The revelry was still going on in the square, but news of the king's trap was slowly making its way through the crowds, and soon there was nobody left – only wreaths of flowers and discarded bottles.

Later, in the palace, Flora lay beside Johnny on one of the huge, soft beds they had been given. Simon and Anna were sitting at their feet. Their own room was next door. Ordinarily they would have leaped up and down on the beds, and splashed in the inviting baths, but now they sat quietly in the fading light.

'I'm not going to cry,' said Flora.

They held hands. 'We can do this,' said Simon. 'The centre of the worlds. We can find it.'

They slept.

Anna snuggled into Simon's side, and Flora and Johnny lay next to each other. Even though they were still far from home, they slept better than they had done for ages, as Simon had found Anna, and Flora had found Johnny.

Their sleep was dreamless.

Deep in the night, when the city, though still confused and frightened, was quiet, a light could be seen burning in one of the towers around the palace, and a figure standing at the window.

It was the tower of the Knight of the Swan. Though his retainers had largely disappeared into the Blindings, fearful of reprisals, one person remained.

He was about fifteen years old, and was tall, slender. He was wearing a long white gown embroidered with feathers. His hands were slim and soft, but his muscles were hard and taut. He was holding a helmet crested with swan's wings. He brought it to his lips and kissed it, his long black hair falling over his bright blue eyes. His name was Cygnet.

'Father,' he whispered. 'Do not fear. I will honour you, and I will find the ones who caused your death, and I will obtain your revenge.'

Something made a noise in the darkness, and the king's two little chattering monkey creatures came scuttling out from where they had been sitting, and nuzzled against his legs. Cygnet placed the helmet on the window sill, and stroked their heads absently.

Then he leaned out of the window, and howled.

Acknowledgements

THANKS ARE DUE to Melissa Hyder, Huxley Ogilvy, Andrea Reece, Tatiana von Preussen, Martin West, and all at Troika.

DISCOVER
THE BEGINNING OF
THE DARKENING PATH

BOOK ONE

THE
BROKEN
KING

WHEN SIMON'S LITTLE sister is mysteriously snatched away to a dark other world, he is sent by a golden messenger on a dizzying quest to get her back. With him is Flora, whose brother has also vanished, and a strange boy who rescues them from a violent attack.

To enter the land of the Broken King they must complete three tasks: Eat the Shadow. Steal the Sun. Break the Air.

But how do they even begin? And what lies in wait for them, in the land of the Broken King?

WHAT LIES
AT THE END OF
THE DARKENING PATH?

BOOK THREE

THE
KING'S
REVENGE

THE BROKEN KING'S trap has been sprung;
nobody can pass between the worlds, and
everything is beginning to decay. Simon and Flora,
reunited with their siblings at last, now face their
most dangerous journey yet: they must go to the
home of the Threefold Goddess.

Lying outside normal space and time, it exists in
the centre of the universe. Perils beset them on all
sides: will they be able to reach her, find out what has
gone wrong, and save all three worlds from dying?
Read the final part of *The Darkening Path* to find out
– coming 2016.

ABOUT THE AUTHOR

PHILIP WOMACK was educated at Lancing and Oriel College, Oxford. *The King's Shadow* is his fourth novel for children. *The Broken King, The Other Book* and *The Liberators* were critically acclaimed and won him comparisons to Alan Garner, John Masefield and M R James.

Philip is a Fellow at First Story, currently being Writer in Residence at St Augustine's C of E High School in Kilburn. He lives in London with his wife, Tatiana von Preussen, and their lurcher puppy.